Oregon Trail Route

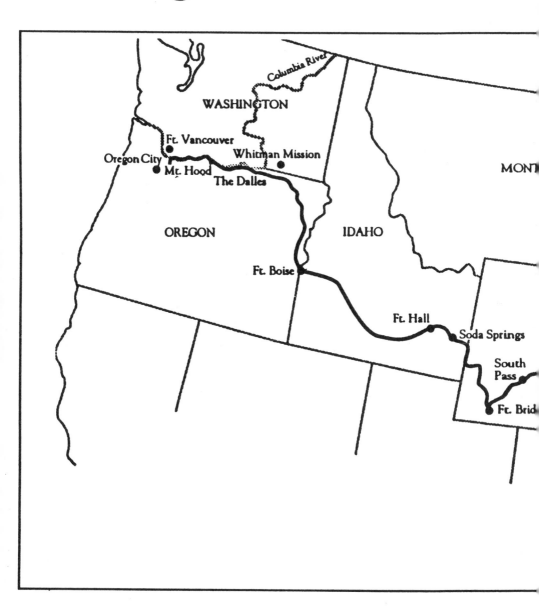

JOURNEY WEST ON THE OREGON TRAIL

Children's Adventures

by

CECILE ALYCE NOLAN

ISBN Number 0-9633168-2-6

Library of Congress Catalog Card Number 93-83792

Rain Dance Publishing Company
P. O. Box 301428
Portland, Oregon 97230

Cover and art work by Michael Gray
Edited by Betty Wilhelm

Although the characters in *Journey West on the Oregon Trail* are fictitious, their experiences are factual and have all been recorded in journals/stories from the Oregon Trail.

*   *   *   *   *

"We must not hope to be mowers,
And to gather the ripe gold ears,
Until we have first been sowers,
And watered the furrows with tears.

It is not just as we take it-
This mythical world of ours;
Life's fields will yield, as we make it,
A harvest of thorns or flowers."

— ALICE CARY

Children of America, give your very best to your family and your country. Remember to guard your heritage so you will be able to harvest flowers!

INTRODUCTION

When I was very young, stories of the Oregon Trail were still filtering down to descendants, still fresh in the minds of some of the old pioneers. Those days have long gone, but many of the old-timers can still recall their parents and grandparents telling intriguing stories about the Oregon Trail in the days before television.

By writing this poignant book, I hope to inform America's children of the trauma, love and fulfillment these courageous pioneers exhibited on their arduous 2000 mile ordeal.

Mrs. Cordelia Kincaid is modeled after my own grandmother who wore heavy corsets with the stays tied so tightly she could barely breathe. Widowed early in her life, she wore black dresses until the day she died. Barely five feet tall, her buxom figure was always held very stiff and proper. She listened to the stories related by her mother who traveled the Oregon Trail, then handed the precious memories down to the rest of the family. The prairie chicken story is one I remember very well. Also, the handkerchief courting dance goes way back to the eighteenth century.

WAGON TRAIN MEMBERS

RACHEL MARIE BRANDON Age 9 — Blonde hair (braided down back), blue eyes. Family came down the Mississippi River by steamboat from Painesville, Ohio. Their wagon rolled off the boat and was lost overboard. The family had to wait at the camp for a replacement wagon. The Brandon family has a pet fox terrier named, Quincy.

SARAH ANN BRANDON (Often called Sarah) Age 14 — Dark blonde hair, blue eyes.

ANDREW BRANDON Age 4 — Known as Baby Andrew (Died on the Oregon Trail.)

HENRY (Hank) BRANDON — Light brown hair, hazel eyes, tall, lean, rugged. Father of Rachel, Sarah Ann, and Andrew.

REBECCAH (Becky) BRANDON — Blonde hair worn in a coronet on top of her head, blue eyes, pleasant, tall, good homemaker. Mother of Rachel, Sarah Ann, and Andrew.

BENJAMIN COLE ELLIOTT (Friends call him Ben) Age 10 — Brown, straggly hair (long), brown eyes. From Scott County, Kentucky.

JONATHAN ELLIOTT Age 15 — Straggly brown hair, hazel eyes. The family owns a very big Conestoga wagon.

SAMUEL ELLIOTT — Owner of the big Conestoga wagon and father of Benjamin and Jonathan. Fair-minded, helpful.

LYDIA ELLIOTT — Mother of Benjamin and Jonathan; devoted, a good friend.

MRS. CORDELIA KINCAID — Widowed, she always wears black and very tight corsets which were the custom of that time in our history. Her spine is always held very straight. She also wears a black bonnet. Her husband died at the camp near Independence, Missouri, and she elected to continue the trip she and her husband had planned. Her big yellow cat named Samson was called Sam. The children on the train call her the "Cat Woman." She always "speaks her mind."

HORACE — A very practical man and very outspoken like Mrs. Kincaid. He was raised on a farm. He takes on the job of protector for Mrs. Kincaid.

ZEKE (Just Zeke...No last name) — As an old time frontiersman and tracker, his job is to scout for the train. After the beaver was decimated in the Oregon Territory, many rugged mountainmen became scouts for the wagon trains going west. He wears fringed, grease-stained buckskin clothing and knee-high moccasins. His rifle is called "Ol' Bess." He chews tobacco and spits frequently. He rides a rugged pinto Indian pony.

CAPTAIN ISAAC QUARLES — Elected Captain of the wagon train because he is firm but fair. He rides a tall bay stallion.

NATHANIAL — Scout for the late-arriving wagon train outside Independence. He is in his early thirties, wears buckskin clothes, and wears his yellow hair down his back. He carries a Hawken rifle and rides a swift black range horse. He is well known on the frontier as having a "good eye" (which means he is an excellent shot!).

JEDEDIAH SIMMONS — Jed joined the train at Chimney Rock after deciding to travel back out to Oregon with the wagon train. He's a retired fur trader from out West; he's just bumming around now. He wears red long johns under his buckskin shirt and has a nervous habit of scratching his neck under the long johns. He wears his black hair, long and straggly, flowing down his back with a beaded Indian headband. His revolver is slung low on his hip, and he carries a tarnished double barreled shotgun in a scabbard attached to his saddle. He either wears or lets hang down his back a worn, flattened hat. In addition, he carries a huge knife at his waist. His knee-high fringed buckskin leggings swish when he walks and a gleaming bear tooth necklace hangs around his neck. Often, he takes out the "makings" and rolls a cigarette. He rides a cantankerous sorrel horse named Darlin'. Jed was known as a "colorful character" in the days of the early West.

DARLIN' — Jed's sorrel mare is golden colored with a straggly white mane and tail. She puts on a good show of being ornery but is really a sweetheart. She is a very light, warm, golden color. She snaps, kicks, and bites at other horses and people she doesn't like and she is an excellent judge of character. She eats anything she can get her mouth near — wood, leather, hair, skin — she's not particular. Darlin' just loves Sarah Ann and Rachel.

1

With a grimy finger Rachel wiped a single tear from her eye. She didn't know if she was crying from loneliness or if the choking dust churned up by hopeful settlers and the confusion of livestock milling about the crowded campgrounds had made her eyes water.

All of her nine happy years had been spent on their farm outside of Painesville, Ohio. Then suddenly, her father had gotten it into his head to undertake a surely impossible journey clear across the whole continent of America! "We're going to 'see the elephant'," he had announced proudly.

Didn't he *know* there were savages out there? She couldn't even begin to think about wolves or snakes. Why, they would have to sleep in a tent, or in a wagon, or heaven forbid, under it on the cold damp ground. Oh, how she would miss her comfortable bed which had already been given to her cousin, Amanda. "Too heavy!" her father had declared with a crooked smile of apology.

She shuddered as she remembered the grisly stories she overheard while climbing in the sycamore tree outside her window back home. Her father and a neighbor had stopped to talk beneath her favorite hiding place to plan their trip to the Oregon Territory. What she overheard still gave her nightmares.

The yellow braid down her back bounced as she shook her head in puzzlement. She stared at the maze of humans and animals trying to live a normal life among wagons, tents, and campfires in a frontier camp bustling with activity. Nearly nine miles from Independence, Missouri, the frenzied camp was considered the frontier and was barely civilized. Horses, cows, mules, and oxen bent their heads trying to find a few scarce blades of grass while bawling their complaints. Excited children ran back and forth fetching water, running errands and playing games. Noisy dogs seemed to run wild. Newcomers camped wherever they could find space while smoke from cooking fires burned their throats and made their eyes water. The offensive stench of so many animals and unwashed humans combined with cooking odors was nearly overpowering.

Quincy, her little brown and white pet fox terrier (named after John Quincy Adams, America's sixth president) was barking frantically at something that caught his attention. His alert, black eyes were fixed on a nearby fight while the hair on his neck bristled in anticipation. Two boys were rolling in the dust, while pounding each other with their dirty fists. A large crowd gathered, egging them on. Rachel recognized one of the bedraggled boys. Once, he had helped her father mend some harness for the oxen. Her eyes widened as she watched his worn, brown homespun trousers rip at the knee. He was using his dirty bare feet to push the larger boy off his prone body. Rip...went the sleeve of his tattered shirt! Rachel felt he needed help since it appeared he was getting the worst of the fight. She knew she had to act fast. It was apparent the smaller boy was no match for his bigger opponent.

"Go get him, Quincy!" Rachel yelled to her pet over the noise of the watching crowd. With a bark of delight, Quincy ran to the youngsters rolling in the dirt, sunk his teeth into a bit of cloth and began to growl viciously. The larger boy glanced up at the tiny dog attacking him, then at the jeering crowd, jumped up

and ran away. Rachel reached down, stroked Quincy's ear and said, "Good boy!"

"Is that your dog?" the grubby boy called to Rachel as he wiped his grimy face with his dirty hands. Jumping to his feet he tried to tidy his appearance by pulling his tattered clothes into some kind of order. With grubby fingers he combed back his shaggy, dark brown hair.

"No, he belongs to my folks, but I think he likes me best," she answered as she carefully examined a loose button on her calico dress.

"I really didn't need any help. I was winning!" he crowed as he grinned shyly at her. "But, thanks, anyway." He pulled a faded handkerchief from his pocket and carefully patted at the blood specks on his swollen lip. Arrogant brown eyes met thickly lashed blue eyes to assess each other. Deciding at the same time to be friends they broke out in fits of laughter.

"Boy, Howdy! Will I catch it when I get back to camp!" he said with a grimace. Sticking out a dirty, blood streaked hand, the brown-eyed charmer said jauntily, "My name's Benjamin Cole Elliott. I'm ten years old and I hail from Scott County, Kentucky. All my friends call me Ben."

Her laughing blue eyes suddenly frowned in disgust as she reached out to grip the offered blood-stained hand. "Glad to meet you, Ben," she said shyly. "I'm Rachel Marie Brandon, from Painesville, Ohio. My mother, father, and older sister, Sarah Ann, whose fourteen, and my little brother, Andrew, are camped right over there under that willow tree. We've been here nearly two weeks, waiting for a wagon to be delivered. We took a riverboat down the Mississippi River from Ohio. During a storm our wagon broke loose and was lost overboard. Papa replaced nearly everything we'll need on the trip except my favorite doll. He said I was much too old for dolls anyway." she confessed wistfully. "Two wagon trains have already left us behind. Papa can't wait to get started."

"Everyone is in such a rush to get going," agreed Ben, nodding his shaggy head. "We arrived late yesterday afternoon. The sun was already down so we had to set up camp in the dark. Papa said it was good practice for the trail. We were told to be here early in May prepared to make the trip. Hey! I know where they're holding a meeting to elect officers. Do you want to go?" Ben asked anxiously. "We can hide so nobody will see us."

Rachel had been lonely since they had reached the camp. She missed her friends and relatives back home. It seemed everyone was too busy to pay much attention to her. It felt good to have a new friend. "Well, I shouldn't, but maybe I won't be missed. Let's go!"

A large group of men, meeting to try to elect officers and adopt rules for the newly formed wagon train, were standing near a stream. Many were dressed in brown or gray homespun clothes. A few dressed in greasy looking buckskins. Their rifles were carelessly slung over their shoulders or braced on the ground at their feet. Most wore their hair hanging loosely down their backs, but others tied it back neatly with a rawhide string. Rachel had heard tales about frontiersmen that would "curdle milk!"

Rachel whispered to Ben, "See that tall man over there with his foot on a tree stump? Papa says he's our guide. I heard Papa and Mama say they were a little afraid of him. There's a story going around camp that he's killed dozens of Indians, and he used to be a fur trader out West. They say he even had an Indian wife! Look, those are animal skins he's wearing!" Rachel declared breathlessly, "and he always carries that gun. They say he talks to it and calls it Ol' Bess!"

One of the emigrants was complaining in a loud whiny voice as he spat tobacco juice on the ground. "Why kaint I join this here train? My mules yonder are as strong as those dumb oxen and a whole lot smarter, too, I'll wager!" As the men joined in the argument, Ben and Rachel leaned on a willow tree near the water's edge to listen.

"What's that piece of paper nailed on that tree? Some kind of notice, I reckon. I can't read so good, Rachel, I had to help out on the farm back in Kentucky when I should have been going to school," Ben said bashfully as he wiggled his bare toes in the dirt and looked at Rachel expectantly.

"I think I can read most of it, Ben. It says:"

WESTWARD BOUND EMIGRANTS!

Emigrants of good character be at INDEPENDENCE, MIS-SOURI, as early in MAY as possible. Campgrounds with water are available about nine miles west of Independence. Wagons will depart for OREGON, CALIFORNIA, or SANTA FE as soon as the grass on the prairie is green enough to sustain livestock. Trading Posts and Blacksmith Shops are in close proximity to the camps so supplies can be obtained if needed. Supplies needed are as follows:

1 heavy wagon covered with double Osnaburg canvas.
Coated well with gutta-percha substance to keep out the rain.

At least 2 yoke of sturdy, dependable oxen between 2-4 years old. Most trains require oxen instead of mules.

YOUR WAGON MUST NOT EXCEED 2500 LBS. FULLY LOADED!

Supplies needed:

flour	spices	nails
bacon	dried vegetables	saws
sugar	frying pans	ox yokes
salt	iron kettles	harness
coffee	coffee pot	spare parts
beans	knives	tools
pepper	baking pans	horseshoes
tea	utensils	extra clothes
cornmeal	tin plates	axle grease
baking soda	buckets	bedding
saleratus	tin reflecting oven	lye soap
oats	skinning knives	sewing supplies
cured meat	water barrels	small personal items
dried fruit	rope	
vinegar	spade	

Livestock: extra oxen, mules, horses, cows, pigs, goats, chickens, dogs
For trading with Indians: tobacco, mirrors, trinkets, beads, cloth, ribbons

BE ON TIME or BE LEFT BEHIND!

7

As Rachel read the notice out loud to her new friend, she stumbled over the word, p-r-o-x-i-m-i-t-y. "I don't know what that word means," she said shyly.

"My family back in Kentucky got a notice just like that one," Ben claimed as he slapped at a mosquito. A loud chorus of "Nays" met their ears as their attention was once more drawn to the crowd of men.

"What did I tell you, Horace, the vote is against takin' your ornery mules to Oregon with this hyar wagon train! Oxen *only* the notice says," one of the men clad in buckskin was explaining. "Now, let's get to the business at hand which is electin' officers and settin' up rules, or we'll never git started. Horace, you'll just have to wait for a wagon train that takes ornery critters or trade your stubborn mules for a yoke of fine oxen, iffen you can!" he added with a grin. "I for one am anxious to take up my land grant out in the Oregon Territory. I heered the Willamette Valley flows with 'milk and honey' and the hills 'abound with deer and elk,'" he announced proudly. "So we need to get back to business and elect a captain to be our leader and get some rules set up, iffen you don't mind!"

The excited men all began to talk at once. Gradually items on the agenda were agreed upon or discarded as unworkable. Items agreed on were: no swearing, no obscene conversations, no stealing, and no immoral conduct allowed on the wagon train. All punishable by expulsion from the train.

As Ben and Rachel crouched behind an old willow tree that hung out over the water and shielded them from view, a small branch drifted down and landed on top of Ben's head. Startled, they both jumped, then broke out in laughter. Ben ran his hand through his unruly hair, grabbed Rachel's hand and began to run, dragging her behind him.

Slowing as they neared the camp, Ben looked at Rachel and asked with a pained expression on his face, "Come and meet my folks. My mother will skin me alive for messing up my clothes. She'll have to work half the night to repair them. It will go easier on me if you're there." At the sign of reluctance on Rachel's face, Ben begged, "Aw, please! Be a friend!"

"Well, alright, but I can only stay a minute."

Stumbling as they made their way past restless animals, smoking campfires, and wagons with sleeping gear protruding into their path, Ben finally stopped at a wagon near the edge of camp.

"Golly," cried Rachel with awe in her voice. "That's really a *BIG* wagon!"

"It's a Conestoga wagon," Ben said with pride in his voice. "They're called 'prairie schooners' because they are as big as a ship. Many say they even look like ships traveling across the rolling prairie. Some of the more experienced Oregon Trail scouts told Pa that this big wagon is much too difficult to maneuver. They told him it was too heavy to lower down the cliffs with ropes. Pa says he's sorry now that he bought this dumb wagon."

"Our new wagon is not as big as yours. After our old wagon fell overboard, my father had to take what was available," Rachel said.

As she spoke, a woman came from behind the wagon with a bundle of folded clothes in her arms. "Benjamin Cole Elliott! What have you done to yourself? Are you hurt?" Concern showed on her pretty face. "Whatever will your father say?" she mumbled as if talking to herself.

"Aw, Ma, don't fuss so. It was only a little ruckus, and he was bigger than me. I'm real sorry I ruined my clothes. But look, I've found a new friend. Meet Rachel, Ma."

"Well, how do, little Missy. Welcome to our temporary home. Will you stay for supper?"

"Thank you kindly, ma'am, but I'm expected home, soon," Rachel answered, a little disappointed.

"Well, I declare! Here comes Jonathan, now. Come here, son, and meet your brother's little friend, Rachel."

Tall for his age, Jonathan at fifteen wore his father's hand-me-down clothes. His callused hand brushed his straggly brown hair out of his hazel eyes, now bright with excitement.

"Welcome, Rachel!" he said as he gave her a friendly smile, then turned with bright eyes toward his mother. "Ma! I've got big news! There's a rumor going around camp that the wagon train leaves tomorrow! Pa sent me to tell you he had to go to a meeting, but he'd be home soon."

"Land sakes!" His mother exclaimed as she dropped her bundle to the ground in dismay. Shaking her head, she said, "I'm not sure we're ready. Will it really happen, son?" Her voice quivering, she spoke hesitantly, "I'm s..so..sort of scared." Jonathan seeing tears come to his mother's eyes, patted her on the shoulder, while he wiped the tears away with the corner of her apron.

"It'll be okay, Ma. You've got me and Pa to take care of you and Benjamin." Jonathan patted his mother's arm to comfort her as he picked up the bundle she had dropped in her excitement. He'd never seen his mother break down like that before. She had always been the strong one in the family, always saying, "That's God's will!" to any disaster that happened.

Embarrassed at such a tender scene, Rachel called out as she turned to run to her own wagon to deliver the news, "See you tomorrow!"

A spectacular sunrise found the make-shift camp bustling with frenzied activity early the next morning. The rumor had been true. An eager council had declared the grass green enough to sustain the livestock and everything was as ready as it would ever be.

Bedlam! Excited men were yoking oxen to the wagons. Loud voices called to friends. Frightened cattle bellowed! Chains jingled. Men and boys yelled and whistled at the animals! Dogs of all sizes ran barking and yipping frantically! Horses whinnied their distress. Whips cracked! Brave women swallowed their fear and hurriedly packed and repacked the wagons. As the hustle and bustle lessened, the captain took charge and gave each wagon a number.

Jonathan's family received number 24. This meant they would be 24th in line. With a grin, Samuel motioned to his son. "Climb up on that seat, son. You'll be doin' the drivin'."

Jonathan's mouth dropped open and his eyes gleamed. "You m-m-mean," he stuttered in his excitement, "I'll be driving the ox team to Oregon?"

"Well, leastways part of the way, son," his father explained. "I'll need to scout and hunt game. You're practically a man at fifteen, and your Ma'll be wanting you to help out. From what I hear about the rigors of the trail out yonder, you'll be needing to grow up fast! Your Ma'll require both of us to help her and Benjamin make it all the way out to Oregon."

Jonathan's mouth stretched into a secret smile as he climbed up on the hard wagon seat and took the reins with eager hands from his father, never dreaming of the magnitude of the task he eagerly accepted. Cracking the whip over the oxen, he called out loudly, "Get up there, Willy Boy! Move on, Flytail! Quit your lollygagging!" as he skillfully drove the team into his family's place in line.

Last minute letters had been written to friends and family. Tearful goodbyes were said to campground friends left behind.

11

Supplies had been checked and rechecked. In blissful ignorance of the hardships awaiting them, each hopeful pioneer watched the Captain as his arm rose in the air. With pride in his voice, shouting as loud as he could over the din, he called, "Let's roll!"

As his arm fell, he nudged his horse to the front of the long column and began to lead a tidal wave of westward rolling humanity on to the promised land.

Jonathan, with a proud grin nearly splitting his face, whispered to himself, "On to the Golden West!" as he followed the wagon in front of him now nearly obscured by clouds of dust.

2

Not everyone was experienced at handling teams. Many women and young boys attempted to do their part as their elated husbands and fathers pranced to and fro on lathered horses. They used any excuse to ride back to town for supplies or to mail forgotten letters. Excitement, joy, or sadness filled each pioneer, but all were bubbling over with enthusiasm. Many oxen not accustomed to each other and crazed by the incessant noise, refused to move. Others bolted in the wrong direction. Inexperienced drivers ran over pot holes breaking axles or shifting poorly packed loads. Some got stuck in mud holes making it necessary to hitch up another yoke of oxen to drag them out. Slowly, the wagon train began to inch forward.

Rachel's family drew number 19 and took their place in the line of scattered clusters of white topped wagons. Her father Henry, not owning a horse, was driving their team of oxen. Her mother Rebeccah, with little four year old Andrew clutched in her arms, sat on the narrow wagon seat beside her husband. Rachel's older sister, Sarah Ann, perched on her knees to better see the excitement while Rachel, holding on for dear life, peered out the back of the wagon. Soon the train slowed again to a crawl.

Sarah Ann's sky blue eyes seemed to swivel in her head. Trying to watch all the frenzied activity at the same time was nearly impossible. Suddenly, she pointed at the wagon ahead, "Look, Ma! Are those pigs?"

The whole family looked through the dust and began to laugh. A very determined mother hog was chasing after five of her baby pigs, grunting her displeasure at their antics.

"Why would anyone take pigs on a 2,000 mile trip?" Rachel asked her parents with disbelief in her voice. As she spoke, a girl about 12 years old jumped out of the wagon ahead and began to coax the pigs, teasing them with an empty bucket. Thinking the bucket contained food, the pigs began to follow the wagon again.

Smiling at how easily the hungry pigs had been tricked, her mother explained, "Girls, owning a hog is better than having gold. It can provide a hungry family with ham, bacon, and sausage. With a little hard work, it will provide cracklings, headcheese, pickled pig's feet, ham hocks, lard for frying, and two very important items, candles and soap. Why, how would I ever keep you children clean without soap?" she laughed as she hugged the children lovingly. "That's why they're trying to take the pigs to Oregon. Let's hope they make it!"

Most able-bodied emigrants were walking beside or behind the wagons by now. Women and young girls pulled their poke bonnets down low on their heads to keep the hot sun from ruining their milky-white complexions. Soon the call was passed down from wagon to wagon. "Nooner!" Each person sighed with relief as the wagons slowed to a halt. Rachel and Sarah Ann helped their mother cook the noon meal, wash the dishes, and repack the wagon. Then they rested and tended to their blistered, sore feet in the time they had left. Soon they were on their way again. The afternoon brought delays, breakdowns, and arguments that resulted in the disorganized wagon train only advancing five miles on their first day.

Two men riding skittish horses, made their way slowly through the wagon train, giving each family a message. Zeke, the caravan's scout, rode a tall pinto, that looked like an Indian pony, with two battered canteens hung over the saddle horn. A tattered, worn bedroll nestled behind the saddle. The rolled edge of the cantle made a perfect place to carry the bedroll.

Zeke (when asked what his last name was, replied that he was "just Zeke") called out to the Brandon family, "Hank, we made pretty fair time, for a first day on the trail, but we need to keep to a schedule, so we'd better make camp now."

Captain Isaac Quarles added, "When we give the signal, follow the wagon ahead, and you'll learn our nightly ritual of pulling the wagons into a corral for safety. These Kansas Indians are well known to run off all the stock they can. The boys can feed and water the livestock while the women cook supper. Then all animals go inside the corral. At eight o'clock, we'll post guards. Someone will let you know when your turn comes around." With a salute of his hand, he whirled his bay stallion and rode to the next wagon.

Delicious smells of biscuits, bacon, and coffee filled the air, mingling with horses sweat, foul smelling dung, and the pungent tar mixture the men used to grease the wagon wheels. People were milling around the camp, making friends, discussing the day's progress, comparing supplies and equipment, and cooing over small children and babies. Someone brought out a fiddle, someone else a banjo and began to play a jolly tune. Soon, feet were tapping, voices were singing, and even though tired, some were dancing.

Rebeccah Brandon leaned over and spoke to Sarah Ann, "Dear, we need some more water for breakfast. Your father is at a meeting, and I must put Andrew down for the night. Will you bring me another bucketful?"

"Oh, sure, Mama, I'll just go get the bucket. There's plenty of daylight left." Sarah Ann assured her mother.

Sarah Ann glanced around anxiously as she made her way down to the river with the bucket. The bank was slippery with mud from all the people and animals getting water. As she bent to dip the bucket in the water, her feet skidded out from under her and she sprawled in the mud. Trying to rise, she clumsily stepped on the hem of her dress and fell kicking and screaming into the river. Suddenly, a strong hand reached down and dragged her up on the bank.

Muddy, wet, miserable, and embarrassed, Sarah sputtered, "T..Th..Thanks! I thought I would surely drown!" Wiping the water and mud from her eyes, she looked up at the young man bending over her and asked, "Who are you?"

With a twinkle in his eyes, trying his best not to laugh, he replied, "I'm Jonathan Boyd Elliott, at your service. At present, that Conestoga wagon over there is my home. I'm pretty sure I met your little sister, Rachel, back at the Independence camp. She and my brat brother, Benjamin, are friends." Grinning, he added with a gleam in his eye, "I think you need some advice on how to carry water. You sure are a clumsy little kid, aren't you? Why, you look like a drowned rat!" Jonathan declared as he grinned devilishly. "You appear to be about twelve. How old are you anyway?" he asked as his long arm reached out over the river and dipped up a bucket of water.

Indignant, Sarah Ann answered, "I'm fourteen. How old are you, Mr. smarty-pants?" Her eyes widened as she spoke, then her hand went to cover her mouth, as she suddenly remembered her mother's advice to always act like a lady. "I'm sorry!" she murmured with downcast eyes, "You probably saved my life." With a little curtsy she said, "Thank you, kind sir!"

A grin brightened Jonathan's face, "Say, you're alright!" he replied. "My grandfather taught me how to carry water. He showed me how to make a pole to carry two pails of water at one time."

"Two pails! Why, I can barely carry one," she cried as she picked up the nearly full bucket sloshing water on the ground.

"Let me make a yoke for you and then you can try it out. I can have it ready by tomorrow morning. Will you meet me here at the river?" pleaded Jonathan.

Sarah Ann picked up the pail, ran a few steps, turned, set the pail down sloshing more water and called back to Jonathan, "I'll be here." Then giggling, she said, "I think you're very nice," and quickly ran back toward the camp.

Dawn came early the next morning. Emigrants still tired from the efforts of the day before, began their chores. Rachel and Sarah Ann helped cook breakfast while their father saw to the livestock. Cornpone, bacon, and coffee smelled delicious in the early morning air.

After eating breakfast, Sarah Ann called to her mother, "I'm going down to the river to get some water."

Her mother shook her head, mumbling to herself, "I thought she got water last night."

Remembering to grab two pails as Jonathan had asked, Sarah Ann ran as fast as she could down the path to the river. Her eyes searched the area for a familiar face. Yes, there stood Jonathan waiting for her, holding a weird looking pole. "Here I am," she called.

Jonathan answered, "I was afraid you wouldn't come. Here's the pole I promised."

Taking the buckets from her, he hooked one on the end of the pole and dipped it full of water from the river. Then did the same with the second pail, setting them down without sloshing a drop. Placing the yoke over her slim shoulders, he reached down, picked up both buckets and hooked them on the ends of the pole. "Do you see how I padded it here, where it fits around your neck?" Jonathan was asking, when they both heard an urgent call from the wagon train. "Let's Roll!"

Sarah Ann turned and began to run cautiously toward the train with her burden. She called back to him giggling as she ran, "I think I like it! Thanks, Jonathan, until you're better paid."

Jonathan took off his battered hat, scratched his head and grinned his pleasure. Just then he remembered the call from the train. "Jimeny Christmas! I'll get skinned if I'm late!" he mumbled to himself as he ran toward his wagon.

The day was a repeat of the day before. Everyone did their best to keep up with the wagons leading the train. The hot, relentless sun beat down on the women and children who often lagged behind the train slapping at pesky mosquitoes. Many had difficulty walking on their blistered feet and swollen ankles. Several minor accidents, a bent wheel, and an Indian scare brought the train to a stop several times during the day. Someone had reported a dust cloud on the horizon, causing a warning cry, "Indians!"

Captain Quarles rode up and down the long column on his dusty bay stallion calming and reassuring everyone. "It was just a dust-devil! You'll be seeing lots of them on this trip."

With a sigh of relief, the weary travelers heard the call, "Time to corral!" Wood had been gathered, fires built, and supper was bubbling in the pots when Zeke rode into camp. He talked with the Captain, then sent word out for a meeting to take place away from the wagons.

Captain Quarles brushed dust from his clothes, slicked back his hair, then held his hand up for quiet, and began to speak. "Men, we made good time today. You all did real good keepin' up. Tomorrow, if we're lucky, we'll be fording the Kansas River, so we'll have to be mighty smart to get the wagons over. It won't be easy."

Zeke stepped up in front of the crowd of men, spat a stream of tobacco juice out of his mouth, adjusted his hat, and drawled,

"We'll be in Sioux and Pawnee country, soon. Iffen we live through that, we'll be goin' through Arapaho and Cheyenne country next. Shoshone and Nez Perce eyes will be watching our every move while we're in their territory. Who knows how the Paiutes and Cayuse will take to us crossing their lands. For several months, we'll be crossing land sacred to the Indians. They may or may not like us being there, so offer them a handout...food and presents...most of you brought trinkets with you. I've lived in their camps, wintered with them, so let me know if there's a ruckus. I'll do my best to handle it. Indians think differently than we do about things. There's no need for trouble, so don't go asking for it!" Worried, and muttering to themselves about the proper way to handle Indians, the men returned to their camp-fires to eat their supper and turn in for the night.

Rachel awoke in distress! She felt a heavy weight in the vicinity of her stomach. What was happening to her? Pulling back the heavy canvas curtain at the back of the wagon, she could see the sky was beginning to lighten. Everyone would soon be up and about, and starting their morning chores. Disturbed at the heaviness she felt, her fingers reached to rub her stomach, coming in contact with a round furry creature. Alarmed, she lifted it up to the light now coming into the wagon. "A cat?" dismayed, she murmured, "It's only a cuddly cat!"

The fat, golden cat opened his green eyes, stretched and meowed his contentment. As she petted the cat, Rachel reached over and shook Sarah Ann awake. Holding one of the cat's paws, she stroked her sister's face with it. Giggling, they began to play with the cat wondering if their father would let them keep it. Soon, they became aware of loud voices coming closer to the wagon.

"Here, Kitty! Kitty! Where are you, Sam? Please come home." called a pleading voice.

Another more familiar voice interrupted saying, "You do understand, Cordelia, we can't hold the train up for Samson, those are the rules. If Samson doesn't show up by the time we have to leave, we'll just have to continue without him," Captain Quarles lectured. "After all, he's just a fool cat."

"Rules or no rules, sir, Samson is all I have left in this world. Here I am next to nowhere...in the middle of to 'hell and gone'...and I will not leave him all by himself to die! Nor will I budge from this spot until Samson comes back to me." Pointing one finger at the Captain's big chest, and drawing herself up to her full five feet, she proclaimed furiously, "And furthermore, my name is Cordelia Kincaid but you, *SIR*, may call me Mrs. Kincaid."

"There's no need to get your dander up, MRS. KINCAID!" proclaimed Captain Quarles as he glared angrily at the little stiff-backed widow, who stared back at him without a blink of her eye. The Captain sighed, shook his head in disgust and walked away.

Mrs. Kincaid's black-clad buxom figure bristled with indignation. The stays of her corset were so tight they often interfered with her breathing, but she refused to loosen them. Her husband had suddenly become ill at the Independence camp and had died. She immediately donned widow's weeds, placed a black bonnet on her head and took up his duties. Refusing to let his death deter her from the journey, she declared that Samson would be her companion and they would continue on the trip to the Oregon Territory.

Captain Quarles had argued saying, "Over my dead body!" but backed down when some of the members offered to drive her wagon and help with the many chores. Most of the driving was done with her own black-gloved hands. With her back straight and stiff, she sat upon the wagon seat refusing to give in to fatigue. Always she behaved as a proper lady, although her language was often a little racy.

Happy when she could be of help to someone, she would call to Zeke as he was riding out for the day's scouting, "Here, sonny, I cooked too much food, again. Take some off my hands so it don't spoil."

Zeke being a loner, kept to himself, away from camp, and did very little cooking. Usually he went without a mid-day meal. Zeke would lean down, take the bundle and politely reply, "Much obliged, Ma'am."

Rachel and Sarah Ann looked at each other and said in unison, "It's the Cat Woman!" Rachel called, "Here's Samson, Mrs. Kincaid, he's been visiting at our wagon. He sure gave me a fright this morning!"

"Oh, you naughty boy, why did you scare your mommy like that? Well, you rascal, what do you have to say for yourself?" she scolded as she lifted him lovingly into her arms.

Sam promptly answered with an annoyed, "Me..ow!" Sarah Ann and Rachel broke out in giggles.

The Captain tipped his hat to the girls peeking out of the wagon and said grumpily, "Tell your Pa there will be a meeting on the banks of the river before we cross over, and we expect him to be there."

3

Midmorning brought the river in sight. Men were already dismantling the first wagons to arrive. Wearing a curious mixture of Indian and western clothes, several young Indian men were talking and using hand signs with Zeke. Often, Zeke would shake his head, frown and speak in guttural sounds. Finally, after much haggling, a deal was agreed upon and the Indians began to help load the first wagon onto a flatboat, that looked more like a raft. Everyone thought $3.00 a wagon was much too expensive. At this rate, they would all be broke by the time they reached Oregon Territory.

As the women unpacked the wagons and hurriedly prepared what was available to eat, the men removed the wagon wheels. With the help of several men they lifted the first wagon onto the flatboat. In the case of the smaller wagons, the Indians poled across the river to the other side, then crews of men put the wheels back on the wagons while the Indians poled back across the river for the rest of the family's gear. But the big Conestoga wagons were too heavy to be poled across. Mules from the remuda were harnessed to the flatboat, then the boat was pulled across the river. Usually it took two trips per wagon. Upsets were frequent and belongings often had to be spread out to dry on the banks of the river.

The Brandon and Elliott wagons were safely across the river when Rebeccah Brandon called the two younger children to pass some time studying. A commotion in the middle of the river caused them to look up from their McGuffey's readers just as Mrs. Kincaid's wagon hit a rock and tipped, causing Samson to go flying out into the river. The unlucky cat disappeared under the whirling, muddy water. A disgruntled Horace, complaining as usual, grabbed Cordelia's arm to prevent her diving in after the unfortunate cat.

"Dag-nab-it, woman!" he growled. "Kaint you ever obey rules? You ain't supposed to ride across with the wagon, you're supposed to wait for the second trip. You pig-headed woman, now look what you've gone and done! You've gone and lost your dad-blamed cat! It's a good thing the Captain had me ride up here with you or we'd be fishing you out of the river."

"Mind your own business, Horace." Cordelia muttered.

Most of the wagons were across the river, assembled, and ready to roll, but had to wait for the last ones to cross, when Mrs. Kincaid approached the captain with her request.

Shaking his head, he replied angrily, "No way, Ma'am. I won't mount a search. That blamed cat is a nuisance!"

"Well, then," Mrs. Kincaid said haughtily, "I won't budge another inch!" Losing his temper, the Captain threw his hat down on the wet river bank and opened his mouth to blast her with a withering reply, when a loud call came from across the river.

"Halloo, Captain Quarles! I've got a message for you!" Splashing toward him was a rider covered in sweat and grime, his lathered black horse obviously exhausted. Dressed in well-worn buckskin with long yellow hair falling down his back, the man appeared to be in his early thirties, obviously an experienced mountainman, assessed Captain Quarles. The pigs finally working up enough courage to attempt crossing the river, ran tumbling and squealing to avoid being stepped on by the nervous horse.

Slapping his hat against his leg to knock off some dust as he dismounted, the exhausted rider nearly fell at the Captain's feet. "Sir, I've been sent to inform you that a contingent of 25 wagons, all from Montgomery County, Illinois, are right behind you and wish to join up with your train. They should arrive at the river in about two hours."

Zeke and some other members had joined the group while the two scouts were talking. The Captain turned to Zeke and said, "Pass the word down the line to make camp back away from the river. We won't corral tonight because we've got company comin'! Tell the men to hobble the livestock while they graze this evening." Turning to glare at Mrs. Kincaid, "Reprieve, Cordelia, Reprieve!" He grumbled as he rode away to tend to his duties, "I'll talk to *YOU* later."

Everyone seemed full of joy that afternoon. Using the river's convenient water supply, the women washed clothes and cooked huge amounts so that the newcomers could have a good meal. Men talked among themselves in groups. They seemed glad there would be more men to help protect the wagon train. Safety in numbers they claimed. Some took the time to read Lansford W. Hastings' book, "Emigrants Guide to Oregon and California," that someone had passed around.

Children ran all over the camp playing tag, tug-of-war, drop the handkerchief, and throwing sticks for their dogs to fetch. Several young girls clapped their hands and sang loudly, "Skip, skip, skip to my Lou. Skip, skip, skip to my Lou. Skip, skip, skip to my Lou. Skip to my Lou, my darling."

Older girls helped with the chores, embroidered, or weaved old strips of material into rag rugs. There were no idle hands. As the afternoon wore on, wagons began to pull into the encampment. Frightened children's faces peered out from behind canvas curtains.

Welcoming women greeted the newcomers and helped them find a campsite, then fed them a hot meal. Most meals consisted of bacon, beans, and coffee. Some women had cooked a stew from dried meat, and a few had made biscuits. Even some desserts magically appeared. Dried peach tapioca pudding, apple fritters, and delicious sweet potato pie. With few men around, the women freely discussed their worries, fears, and complaints. Most of the male members of the wagon train were still on the bank of the river assisting the new arrivals.

Cordelia walked up and down the river bank with a worried frown on her weathered face, watching and hoping she would see some sign of her cat, Samson. Jonathan had borrowed his father's horse and had gone downstream with some other young boys to search. After one look at Mrs. Kincaid's glum face, they thought they should do something to help find Samson. No trace of the luckless cat could be found.

After a long tiring day, the last wagon was being rafted across. All the Indians had been paid with whatever they had demanded. Some wanted money, some wanted food, but most demanded men's shirts. The more colorful the shirt, the better. Everyone watched as the last raft came to the landing. Zeke and Captain Quarles rode their tired horses beside the raft with big grins on their faces as water splashed everywhere. Just before the raft reached the shore, a bit of yellow fluff could be seen sitting on the raft calmly washing his face, like nothing at all had happened. It seemed that Samson had suddenly appeared as the last raft was departing and had nonchalantly jumped on board.

"Don't that beat all!" exclaimed Horace who had been keeping a close eye on Mrs. Kincaid. Reaching out a long, skinny arm, he snatched the fat, startled cat by the scruff of his neck and deposited him in Cordelia's waiting arms.

Dismounting, a smiling Captain Quarles patted Mrs. Kincaid's shoulder and said, "Better put a string around Samson's neck and tie him to the wagon seat. It's going to be a long trip and he's using up too many of his nine lives." Everyone laughed and started to drift back to the camp to show the newcomers where to settle for the rest of the night.

Early morning brought pandemonium as shouting and horses whinnying their distress, awoke the sleeping camp. Hastily grabbing clothes and putting them on as they ran to check on the commotion, the men emerged from their wagons in time to watch as a group of hostile Indians ran off several valuable horses. Whooping and hollering and waving Indian blankets to frighten the horses, they rode in full view of the terrified people on the train. The women drew back in fear at the sight of stripes painted on faces and bows and arrows slung over naked shoulders. Unearthly Indian yells echoed in their ears as horses, and Indians brandishing feathered lances in the air, disappeared into a cloud of dust.

Zeke yelled to Captain Quarles, "Get the train moving. We'll go after the horses. Don't wait for breakfast, we can't take a chance on an attack! This raid could be a diversionary tactic to catch us short handed, so be on your guard. We'll catch up with you later!" Several men mounted their eager horses and the party rode off in a dust cloud.

Making haste all morning, but not having seen any more sign of Indians, the train stopped for a nooner. No fires were lit as they were still on alert. Soon a party of men were seen approaching from a distance. As the horsemen neared camp, a few riderless horses were noticed galloping alongside the mounted riders. A cheer went up from the emigrants. At least the search party had retrieved a few horses. Several women rushed out to greet the returning heroes with food and coffee for the dusty, tired group.

The hot prairie sun beat down on the weary caravan as some rode, but many more walked. Their Captain had insisted that everyone who could, walk either beside their wagons or behind the train. He explained that the oxen needed special care if they were to get the emigrants over the Rockies and through the rugged Snake River Canyons. Many women with their calico poke bonnets pulled low over their eyes preferred to walk behind the train. With no one to notice, they could pull their long skirts up between their legs and hook them under their belt. It looked as if they were wearing pants, which would be much more comfortable than a huge skirt and many petticoats. So much cooler, too.

Modesty prevented them from showing their legs so they preferred the dust cloud that followed the train to hide their shyness. Carrying leafy willow switches they slapped at mosquitoes that bit any exposed area, making welts and red sore spots that were slow to heal. Often they would stop walking, shift a baby or a water canteen to ease a sore arm, remove their sunbonnets and wipe sweat from their necks and faces with a handkerchief or an old rag. Then, with a sigh and a cautious glance around, they would begin their slow tread again.

As afternoon wore on, the white fluffy clouds began to disappear. The hot sun hid its face behind ominous dark clouds. Zeke came riding down the long column calling to the walkers, "Get back to your wagons, quickly! There's a big storm comin'! Cover everything you can. It's going to rain hard!" Already a few sprinkles showed on his dusty clothes as he wheeled his horse and cantered to the next wagon to deliver his message.

Each person scampered to his wagon and began to make preparations for the rain. Some had rain slickers, but most did not. Soon the dusty trail that passed for a road was a sea of mud. The horses slithered and slipped in the slimy mess, but the surefooted oxen plodded on. The Brandon family huddled together under the white canvas cover and shivered with the cold. Rachel and Sarah Ann set buckets under the leaks in the canvas roof. "We can use the rain water to wash our hair," their mother joked with a crooked smile crinkling her face.

Soon the call came down through the wagons, "Corral for the night! Make camp as best you can!" After much confusion, because the new train members did not know their place in the corral, the camp was made secure. Cold, wet, weary pioneers getting a taste of what their trip would be like, made their beds in any dry place they could find.

Some women attempted to make a fire, but the water poured down from the sky and put out the fires. This fierce thunderstorm contained torrents of rain and high winds. Lanterns flickered out over the camp as the hungry settlers and their stock settled down for a wet cold night without any supper.

A hard gust of wind blew the cover off of one wagon, soaking everything inside. Thunder rumbled and lightning flashed off and on during the night. Shivering guards stood at their posts watching for marauding Indians.

Late that night the rains stopped. Damp emigrants emerged from their wagons as the dawn began to brighten the sky. Hungry, they looked for some dry fuel that would burn so they could cook food and dry out their clothes. Nothing! Everything was soaked. Rebeccah Brandon looked out of the wagon at the dismal faces of her family and made up her mind.

"Give me a hand here, Hank," she called to her husband. "Take this old rocking chair out and break it up for fuel."

"But, Ma," complained Sarah Ann. "You know how much you love that old rocking chair. I still remember the commotion you raised when Pa said you couldn't bring it on this trip. Why, you always said you would never part with that old chair because you rocked your babies in it."

"Oh, land's sakes, what a fuss!" Becky muttered, "Get the ax, Hank, my babies are nearly grown."

With a frown on his face Hank chopped up the chair and soon had a blazing fire going. He glanced over at his wife who wiped away a tear that slid down her face with the corner of her apron. "Thunderation!" he muttered under his breath, as he grimaced and scowled at the wet surroundings.

Clothes were dried, breakfasts were cooked, the stock was fed and hitched to the wagon, and the emigrants were ready to start when the call came down the line, "Let's roll!"

Day after weary day went by as the train progressed slowly across the desolate prairie. Many accidents plagued the procession, and slowed it to a crawl. Too often the extra horses following the train in the remuda, ran off and the wagons had to wait for their return, *IF* they could be found. Each member had his own ideas about how the train should proceed. One argument that raged on was the issue of whether or not to rest on Sunday. Captain Quarles and Zeke, joined by Nathanial, who was the scout for the new members to the caravan, agreed they must not stop to rest on Sunday. Everyone should remember that reaching their destination safely, and as fast as was prudent, was still their goal. But, the opposition demanded Sunday rest. A meeting was held to discuss the matter and try to come to an amiable conclusion. After spirited arguments both for and against the Sunday rest, a vote was taken and tallied. It was nearly a tie.

"What do we do now to solve this problem?" everyone was muttering.

Nathanial spoke very quietly, "I have a solution." Heads turned to face the young scout.

"Well, speak up thar, young'un, iffen you got somethin' to say!" called out Horace.

The men nodded their agreement as Nathanial explained, "It's a simple solution. Split up the train!"

Everyone began to voice an opinion, some agreeing, some shaking their heads in disagreement. Captain Quarles held up his hand to quiet them. "Wait a minute, men. Let's give this idea some thought. The plan has some merit," he agreed. "We all know that some wagons move at a slower pace than others. Even the livestock slow us down. Many wagons have to stop to rest the slow moving milk cows tied behind. We've had several delays with sick or injured members. On the positive side, we have two experienced scouts, so all we would be required to do is elect a second captain," he explained as his eyes scanned the crowd in hopes of finding approval of his plan. "Soon, we'll arrive at the banks of the Blue River. If the river is swollen, the crossing can be difficult. Many frontiersmen claim that after you cross the Blue and the Sweetwater, you are man enough to be accepted into America's frontier. Then you can hold your head up with pride among the infamous mountainmen who explored this wild land by trapping beaver and making maps of the area. Let's wait until we cross the Blue to make the decision about the Sunday Train. Alright, men?"

A chorus of "Yays!" greeted his question, as the men considering the meeting over, began to pull out their makings or put a chaw of tobacco in their mouths. Some took advantage of the time away from their families to clean and oil their guns while they chatted about events on the trail.

Several more days of tortuous travel brought them to the banks of the Blue. The recent rain had swollen the river as the Captain had feared. Sullen Indians eagerly awaited the arrival of the wagon trains to be ferried across on the fragile looking rafts. Women helped unload the wagons so they could be loaded onto the rafts, built fires, cooked food, washed clothes, and entertained their neglected children. Men busied themselves unloading, removing wheels, and swapping stories. The pigs busily rooted on the river bank searching for tasty roots. Barking dogs chased each other around the camp. A contented Samson, snoozing in the sun, was tied to the wagon seat. Most of the children were given chores to keep them busy.

Rebeccah combed and braided Rachel's rebellious hair. Sarah Ann tended to her own hair each morning. Sometimes she braided it, but when she was feeling grown up she just let it fall down her back and tied it with a well worn ribbon. In the rush to get under way Rachel's hair was often neglected. Sarah Ann or her mother brushed Rachel's hair as often as they could, to keep it from becoming infected with lice.

Rachel's wagon, number 19, was safely across without mishap. While a crew of men worked to put the wheels back on the wagon, she and Sarah Ann waited on the riverbank to watch number 24, the Elliott's wagon, cross the swiftly moving stream. As the raft neared midway the Indians lost control of the raft as it swirled in the current. Ben tripped on a rope, and fell overboard as the Indians quickly brought the craft under control. Rachel screamed as she saw Ben disappear in the raging water. The watchers on shore gasped in disbelief. Nathanial, astride his swift, black, range horse, rushed downstream, whipping his horse for more speed. Benjamin surfaced reaching out his arms to grab hold of anything to save himself.

A lasso whipped through the air, and went sailing over Ben's head. He grabbed for it and held on for dear life. As Nathanial began to reel him in like a fish on a line, cheers and applause were heard from the shore. Jonathan ran, splashing through the shallow water and grabbed his brother, dragging him up onto the bank. Several men rolled him over a barrel as dirty river water gushed out of his mouth. Ben coughed and sputtered and gradually came back to life.

Samuel dashed up, grabbed his dripping son in his arms, hugged him tightly and exclaimed, "Thank God the Blue threw you back, son!" Everyone laughed and slapped each other on the back to relieve the tension, then went back to the business of getting the rest of the wagons across.

A very wobbly Benjamin rolled to his feet, shook the water from his hair and reached out a trembling hand to Nathanial. With a squeaky voice Ben managed to say, "Th.. an..ks, Nate! I guess you've heard the old saying? Well, I swear, it's true. I'll be your slave for life!"

4

Zeke and Nathanial rode out to scout the area early next morning. They hoped to bring back some fresh meat for their provisions were getting low. Zeke confessed his concern to Nate about the Indian sign he had seen.

"I don't expect these are Kansas Indians," explained Zeke, "because the sign appears to be Pawnee. If so, they're not friendly like the Kansas, Nate."

"I've heered some pretty bad things about the Pawnee," Nate agreed, while his eyes searched the horizon for sign of game or Indians. "We'll soon be enterin' Nebraska Territory. That's what some folks call this part of the frontier."

"We'll have to post more guards at night and keep a sharp look out during the day," agreed Zeke. "What's more, we'll have two trains to watch out for now. Some of those folks are bound and determined to have their Sunday rest, even though it means they might never make it to Oregon. I agreed we'd split the train after we crossed the Blue River. We'll make two corrals tonight, one for the slower folks and one for the faster wagons. Most of the folks that came with you, Nate, have cows and chickens that slow them down, so I'll have to call on you to guide the slower train. I hate to ask this of you since they will have less chance of making it."

"Maybe we won't be too far behind, Zeke. I'll do my best to hurry them along." As he kicked his black horse into a trot, he called back to his friend, "Let's go check out that grove of trees over yonder."

Late that afternoon the two hunters rode hard back to the train. Nate had a big buck deer slung over the back of his skittish horse. Most horses did not like the smell of blood. Zeke had teased the younger scout about his "young eyes" that could sight down a rifle barrel, laughingly saying he himself was better at finding Indian sign. Dismounting to rest their horses, they hailed Captain Quarles. After relaying information about the Indian danger to the Captain, they began skinning the deer. Finished with the skinning, the three men rode to the front of the column to warn the train of impending danger.

Captain Quarles called several men away from the train and told them, "Men, we're going to make a wide swing to the south, beginning right now. Zeke and Nate found sign of a Pawnee hunting party to the north of hyar. About twenty warriors strong. We don't want to meet up with them iffen we can avoid it. We've got about two hours until time to camp. Let's get crackin'."

Lanterns swayed, water sloshed from barrels, wagons creaked and shuddered, crates of squawking chickens rocked, and cows bellowed their fright as the train made haste to avoid any contact with the Indians. A Pawnee hunting party could turn nasty. Whips cracked over the oxen's heads. Animals had to run to keep up.

Quincy's short legs were tiring fast. His tongue lolled out of the side of his mouth dripping with saliva, while his round black eyes bulged. Zeke rode his lathered horse up and down the column making sure there were no laggards left behind. His weathered eyes scanned the horizon, then swung back to the train, alert for any sign of trouble. Seeing the little dog was in distress, he rode up beside him, bent and swept him up in his arms. Kicking his horse into a cantor, he rode up to the Brandon wagon and called, "Rachel, take Quincy. His little legs are too short to keep up with the train."

Reaching out her arms, she gave her pet a hug, and said, "Thanks, Mr. Zeke. Thanks a lot!"

Giving her a salute, he replied, "Remember, Rachel, it's just plain Zeke."

That evening children gathered wood for the cooking fires, then fed and watered the livestock as fast as they could, because darkness was nearly upon them. Their scouts had pushed them as fast as the oxen could go in order to distance themselves from the Pawnee hunting party. Zeke assured the men they could easily find the trail again tomorrow.

"Tonight we'll keep the fires low and keep our talkin' to a whisper, and get an early start in the mornin'. We'll all be doin' double duty tonight." Zeke swung Ol' Bess over his shoulder, spat tobacco juice at a twig on the ground and called back, "I'll take first guard duty. The rest of you turn in and get some sleep."

At first light, the sleepy camp made their plans to split the train into two caravans. After breakfast, Zeke positioned himself on his horse in the middle of the path, calling out. "Sunday rest folks turn to the left...Hurry on to Oregon folks turn to the right." As each wagon pulled into the line of their choosing, two trains began to emerge.

Captain Quarles called to the Oregon folks, "Let's roll!"

With a goodby wave to the families he felt he might never see again, Zeke rode out to help the Captain lead the Oregon train. As scout, his first job was to find the trail they had hurriedly left the day before.

Back on the trail, there was no sign of the Pawnee hunting party. The lead train could travel much faster now that some of the dawdlers had opted for the slower train. Bleak faces looked out from the wagons at the seemingly endless prairie. The vastness of the land was overwhelming. It appeared to rise and fall like ocean waves. Masses of wildflowers dotted the rolling landscape, their delicate heads dancing in the gentle breeze. The freshness of the day and the bright sunshine soon dispelled some of their gloom.

But, grim reality faced them now. The close call with the Indians and the loss of friends, made them more aware of possible impending disasters. As each day passed they slowly began to regain their good humor.

Nate was true to his word, for he kept the second train close behind until the Sunday rest day. Then the procession began to drop back out of sight. Each train had its own troubles to deal with every day. Breakdowns were common, arguments were frequent, and much of their food supply was spoiling. Many women found their bacon was growing a hairy substance on its surface. It was green mold that must be scraped off to make the food edible. Often, there wasn't enough time to finish cooking the stew or beans so that the meal had to be eaten half raw. Most of the cured ham and corned beef had been used up long ago. Tempers were growing short.

All the families who had brought milk cows that were fresh, had joined the slower train, so the folks on the faster train had no butter to eat. The ingenious women had put the cream in the churn and had let the wagon's swaying motion make butter, then had shared with their fellow travelers.

Rachel's family had adapted to living in a wagon and dealing with the constant hazards that challenged them on a daily basis. Often, Sarah Ann was called on to drive the ox team while her mother and father took a break from driving the stubborn oxen. The rest of the family walked beside or behind the lurching wagon. As they walked, Rebeccah rubbed some salve into her husband's hands. Constant handling of the reins had caused rough, raw calluses on his big hands. Mrs. Kincaid had suggested the remedy after noticing that Hank's hands needed doctoring. Her own homemade salve would do nicely, since nearly everything the Brandons owned had been lost when their wagon had gone overboard in the Mississippi River. Many of those belongings could never be replaced.

Sarah Ann's little brother, Andrew, was waking up from his nap. The swaying of the wagon made him sleepy, so he napped often. At four years old his little legs couldn't carry him very far. Everyone loved Baby Andrew and spoiled him dreadfully.

"Mummy, Mummy," he called as he began to awaken. He climbed from his pallet onto the wagon seat looking around with big round eyes. "Where's Mummy?" he whined as he began to lean out of the wagon. Distracted from her driving, Sarah Ann reached over to grab at his sleeve, when suddenly the wagon lurched as it ran over a rock on the trail, and Baby Andrew fell over the side.

"Whoa!" Sarah shouted as she pulled back on the reins, "Whoa, there, Willy Boy! Whoa, Flytail!" Struggling with the team of stubborn oxen, she finally brought them to a halt. Hastily tying the lines around the brake handle she jumped down. The sight that met her eyes sickened her. Baby Andrew lay crumpled on the ground with her mother and father huddled over him. By now, other wagons had stopped and people were running toward them to help. Sarah Ann's head buzzed with bits of conversation she heard, "Wagon wheels ran over him... crushed...get the doctor...is he dead?"

Captain Quarles was called and took charge. Baby Andrew was alive...barely!

Despite the love that was showered on Baby Andrew and the family, he only lived four days. A pallet had been made for him in the doctor's wagon so he would have constant care. The Brandon family was in anguish. Rebeccah sobbed constantly, begging her husband to take her back home.

"Please, Hank, if you love me, you'll take me home to my mother," she cried, wringing her handkerchief with her hands. "I can't take the rest of the children any further to die in that horrible wilderness!"

"Calm yourself Becky dearest," he said, as he patted her tenderly. "Come and lie down in the wagon awhile, and try to get some sleep. The wagon train can't, no, won't turn around and go back to Missouri. We're committed for the duration. We were well aware there would be hardships before we started. Now is not the time to give up. We must keep moving," he soothed her with the gentle sound of his voice as his own heart was breaking.

Of course the wagon train must keep moving, no matter what happened, no matter that lives were shattered. Arriving at their Oregon destination before the terrible winter weather covered everything with snow was the main concern. It seemed that nothing else mattered to the emigrants.

Mr. Brandon emptied a wooden box, sanded it smooth, wrapped his son's poor broken body in a blanket and placed it in the box. Zeke and some of the men had dug a shallow grave and gathered rocks to cover it, so no animals could dig up the tiny body. A brief ceremony was held, then the rocks were piled on top. Captain Quarles had fashioned a small wooden cross with his knife, then Zeke scratched words that read, "Andrew Brandon...4...Much loved." Rachel's father pushed the cross down into the cairn of rocks and with tears streaming down their faces, family and friends said their goodbyes. From the distance a heartbreaking call was heard, "Let's roll!"

Each day Sarah Ann's ache lessened a little. She felt guilty for causing Baby Andrew's death. If only she had been able to catch Andrew...if only she had seen the rock in the trail...if only she could have stopped in time...if only she hadn't been driving. Crazy thoughts whirled around in her head. Each day the family chores kept her so busy that she had little time to brood on her imagined guilt. The grim look of misery never left the family's eyes, but gradually their lives returned to normal.

Hot blistering sunshine beat down on weary heads, dust whirled as they walked, choking already parched throats. Water had been rationed days ago. Only a sip of warm water from the canteen was allowed. Water barrels were nearly empty. The wagons were now rotating their positions daily. Last one to corral at night was first one out in the morning. Jonathan was driving the last wagon while Rachel and Sarah Ann walked nearby. Off in the distance a rider could be seen, his horse kicking up dust. Jonathan shaded his eyes with his hand and called out to the two girls, "It looks like Nate's black horse, but I can't tell who's riding him, yet."

Soon Nate emerged out of the dust cloud. "Whew!" he sighed as he slapped his hat on his knee to dislodge some of the dust. He reined in his tired horse, then took the bandanna he wore around his neck, and wiped the sweat from his face.

"Boy, howdy! It sure is hot and dry, ain't it? Got a sip of water for a parched man?" Sarah Ann looked at Jonathan, his eyes met hers and he nodded. She went to the nearly dry barrel and got Nate a small dipper of precious water. After all, hadn't he saved Benjamin's life.

"What brings you this far away from the Sunday Train, Nathanial?" Jonathan asked as he urged the oxen to catch up to the wagon ahead.

"We..ll, I really need to talk to Captain Quarles, but I reckon it won't do no harm to tell you folks. We got sickness on the train. Don't know what kind yet. Some say prairie fever, or camp fever, but others are claiming it's cholera." The young people all gasped at the mention of the dreaded disease.

"Surely not, Mr. Nate," exclaimed Sarah Ann, "why, back home we all had summer fevers that didn't last very long a'tall.

Mamma would dose us with Castor Oil and we'd be up on our feet in no time."

"Folks been dosing this sickness with sulphur and molasses. Don't seem to be doin' much good, though. The captain of the train made the wagons with the sick folks drop back away from the others, and travel by themselves, until they either die, or get well. Seems kind of drastic, but he says it's necessary to protect the rest of the members. Well, I've got to do some traveling after I talk to the Captain. See y'all!" Nate drawled as he wiped his sweaty brow, donned his floppy western hat and rode off looking for the Captain.

Nathanial, Zeke, and Captain Quarles held a lengthy meeting. The severe drought, Baby Andrew's death, the scare of the dreaded cholera disease were all discussed. It was agreed the word, cholera, would not be mentioned. The mere hint of the word could cause panic. Soon other men joined the discussion and talked of Indians, hunting game, the Oregon Territory, which route to take, families and friends, and soon had them laughing and in a better mood. Nathanial, tucked his Hawken rifle under his arm, mounted his dusty black horse, and with a salute and a wistful look at his friends, began the journey back to the Sunday Train and his duties.

Nebraska Territory was buffalo country. The desolate prairie had no trees, therefore no wood for cooking fires. For days the children had been picking up dried buffalo dung for firewood. They laughingly called them chips. At first the girls begged off, groaning their disgust at having to handle something so gross. But, gradually they became accustomed to the chips and grudgingly joined the boys in the chore. As yet no buffalo had been sighted. Then one day a huge dust cloud was seen in the distance. "Indians!" someone shouted. Fear struck the train.

A shout came down the long column, "Halt the train!" Zeke was riding his lathered horse from the opposite direction. Horses

reared and whinnied their distress, wagons were driven out of line in panic.

"Halt, I say!" Zeke yelled above the din. "Halt! It's a herd of buffalo, not Indians! Stop the wagons until we can discover which way they're goin'. If they come this direction, nothin' can save us. Those fool buffalo will run right over our wagons." Zeke whirled his horse and rode out from the stalled wagon train to where Captain Quarles waited, sitting quietly on his horse. Shading his eyes with his hands, he scanned the horizon. The pioneers watched anxiously for the signal that would tell them to move as fast as they could either north or south or to stay put. One rifle shot meant north, two meant south, and silence meant stay put. Time seemed to stand still, as they watched and waited.

Silence....

A cheer went up from the grateful people, as their jubilant leaders rode happily back to the wagons.

Horace, driving Mrs. Kincaid's rig as usual, declared, "Don't that beat all!"

As the dust cloud approached parallel to the train, an occasional buffalo could be glimpsed through the dust. They had huge, black, shaggy heads and big shoulders with scruffy tufts of fur hanging all over them. The roar of bellowing buffalo, and the drum of hooves beating the ground, made the spectator's ears ache. The ground trembled and shook with the passage of thousands of buffalo. Everyone noticed the noisy beasts seemed to be traveling in a straight line.

"Why is that?" someone called out to Zeke.

Having traveled across the prairie many times in his frontier days, Zeke had seen many buffalo herds and knew the most about the habits of the wandering buffalo.

"We..ll," he drawled, "It's sort of like your children playing follow-the-leader. Those buffalo kaint see too good, so they set their eyes on the leader and follow wherever he goes. Iffen he runs off a cliff, I reckon they will, too. I've seen thousands of dead buffalo at the bottom of a ravine. They'll run over anythin' in their way. Nothin' will make them swerve until they've a mind to. That's why we were holdin' our breaths until we could tell which way they were going. We was real lucky this time."

The call came down the column of white topped wagons, "Let's roll!"

5

As the animals plodded along in the sweltering heat, whispers began to be heard. "Platte...Platte river ahead." This message was a hallmark in their journey. To reach the Platte River, was one of their primary goals. They would follow it more than 300 miles before they branched off in their westward quest. They remembered stories of how the Indians and frontiersmen called it the "flat" because of it's shallow depth. Seasoned mountainmen referring to the infamous river Platte, had declared, "It's too thin to plow and too thick to drink!"

Many thought it was only an inch deep in many places. In truth, it was a dangerous river, full of sandbars, whirlpools, rapids, snags, floating logs, sometimes high water, sometimes low water. And always hidden to the eye, quicksand. A few straggly willow trees lined its banks.

A hushed warning came down through the ranks to keep the stock under tight control. The long drought had made the emigrants edgy and the livestock skittish. Now the smell of water nearby was causing panic among the livestock, who wanted to break their restraints and run to the water. Many thirsty horses, mules, and oxen, following the train in a remuda, broke away and rushed to the water. They swept past the wagons, causing some drivers to lose control of their ox teams. Several wagons overturned, spilling possessions, causing some injuries to live-stock and emigrants. Other oxen, running out of control, dragged the wagons into the middle of the Platte River before stopping. Those on horseback, unable to halt their spirited horses, arrived in time to rescue the drivers stranded in the middle of the river.

Rescuing the oxen and other livestock was another matter. Many were already stuck fast in quicksand and were being sucked down. Weary oxen stood in the water, stranded in their harnesses, which needed to be cut off before they could be rescued. Tired men on horseback worked their lassos as quickly as they could, but often two or three lassos were needed to drag out each an-imal. Several drowned before the exhausted men could reach them. Cuts, scrapes, broken legs, and sprains occurred and were attended to as soon as possible.

Pulling the mired wagons from the river required super-human strength. Scraggly men stood in muddy water and heaved and pushed, while teams of weary oxen pulled from the bank. Finally, the last wagon was dragged from the quagmire and stood forlornly on the muddied banks of the Platte River.

Men, women, and children left to attend the nearly aban-doned wagons, brought buckets of water for the livestock held back from rushing headlong to the river. Older children walked the thirsty livestock one by one to the river to drink. As the situation calmed, the women and older girls began to set up camp and cook a meal for the exhausted men. Everyone agreed this was the worst day on the trail...so far!

Zeke heard a call as he walked exhausted through the camp wiping the water from his face with the tail of his shirt, "Zeke, old buddy, come and take supper with us tonight." Samuel, with his arm around his wife Lydia, stood beckoning to him in the firelight.

"Yes, siree, I do believe I am a mite hungry! I'm much obliged, folks," he answered as he rubbed his empty stomach.

"We'll be laying over tomorrow. There's much to do to get the wagons ready to roll."

Gradually the camp quieted, campfires died down and lanterns and candles flickered out.

Everyone used the needed rest day to their own advantage. Children, too young for chores, ran and screamed their joy, played games and napped. Mothers used their time wisely by washing clothes at the river on scrub boards, refilling their water containers, and cooking what food was available.

Older children well aware of their responsibilities, gathered buffalo chips, tended the younger children and caught up on their schooling. McGuffey's readers were brought out, and in some cases dried off. While children read, and learned to cipher, mothers mixed corn bread, baked biscuits, stirred stew, soaked dried apples for dessert and gossiped among themselves.

Early that morning the hunters had gone out to find deer or elk, and unable to find larger game, brought back some smaller animals to clean. Some of the women not recognizing the meat, asked what kind of game it was.

"Prairie chicken!" laughingly came the answer.

"What kind of animal is that?"

"Anything that moves!" came the reply.

"But...."

"Don't ask!"

"Bosh!" muttered Cordelia, "I don't give diddly-squat what it is. I'm hungry enough to eat a horse!" The men were pointing, slapping each other on the back and breaking up with laughter. Amazed women looked at each other, shrugged, and began cooking the strange looking meat for supper.

"Prairie chicken, indeed!" one lady muttered.

A new day began at 4 a.m. sharp. Sleepy emigrants emerged from their cramped sleeping arrangements to begin their morning chores. Each morning children had to be washed and dressed in whatever was the cleanest and had been mended. Grown-ups had to get themselves washed and dressed before the chores began. Breakfast must be cooked, eaten, the dishes washed, and the supplies repacked. Everyone had to be ready for the 7 o'clock call or risk being left behind in the wilderness. Only the Captain's order could halt or delay the train.

Five hours later, they would stop for an hour long "Nooner" then back on the trail for another five grueling hours, until time to corral the wagons for the night. This rigid schedule sapped the strength from many emigrants whose health had not been strong before they attempted the pilgrimage. Older family members, many in poor health were encouraged to make the trip in hopes their health would improve. These novice pioneers felt their new life in the Willamette Valley would be well worth all the hardships they would have to endure. Many felt freedom from taxation, and rich soil that produced good crops, would give new incentives to their ailing relatives. They felt that good food, such as fresh fish and game, could revitalize their failing health. Instead, their loved one's failing energy waned daily while traveling mile after mile, day after weary day. Most did not live to see the "Promised Land," but perished and were buried along the trail.

"Let's roll," came the call, as refreshed travelers began the long trek beside the Platte River.

Women wearing sunbonnets to protect their heads from the heat, and aprons to protect their clothes from the dust, walked near the wagons. Willow leaf switches flicked back and forth to keep mosquitoes away. After the Pawnee Indian scare they felt safer walking closer to the wagons. Uppermost in their minds after the unpleasant encounter with the Platte River was the news that Captain Quarles had just delivered to them early this morning. They would have to cross that monstrous Platte River several times during their 300 mile trek. The river would be used as a guide for their westward journey and would keep them from dying of thirst.

Several uneventful days passed. A few sprained ankles, some problems with ailing livestock, and other minor inconveniences plagued the train. Rebeccah, already feeling depressed because of Baby Andrew's death, came down with dysentery. Many folks on the train were suffering the same complaint. A committee, embarrassed at discussing something of such a personal nature, went to Zeke with the problem. He rode in at sundown after putting over 12 hours in the saddle to see them waiting to talk to him. The spokesman for the committee put it to him as delicately as possible. Zeke lifted the well worn saddle from his weary horse and answered as he began to wipe the pinto with an old cloth, "Best thing to do is boil yore drinkin' water. The water from the Platte ain't very clean. There's dead animals in the water, and no rocks in the bottom to clean the water as it runs downstream. Remind yore ladies to fetch their buckets of drinkin' water *ABOVE* any dead carcass laying there rotting in the river. You folks just ain't used to all these here new germs, yet. That's all there is to it."

He continued wiping down his sweaty horse and getting the weary animal ready for the night. A frontiersman considered the welfare of his horse more important than his own comfort.

Rachel and Sarah Ann were also getting ready for the night. They had asked their mother to let them use the lantern for a few minutes inside the wagon. Everyone was well aware of the need for caution with fire, for all of their worldly goods could be wiped out in minutes and they would be destitute on the frightening prairie.

Rachel reached up to the pocket that had been sewed onto the canvas cover and brought down needle and thread. She stretched up to another pocket and took out a pair of scissors.

51

She and Sarah Ann had helped their mother sew pockets inside the canvas cover. Many small items were kept there so they would be easy to find. Herbs, seeds for planting, and spices were just a few. Larger pockets held schoolbooks, slates, and soap. Various hooks held ropes, canteens, coats, shawls, sunbonnets, and the men's extra hats. The loaded sixteen shot Henry repeating rifle hung above the wagon seat ready for any emergency. Her father, nicknamed Hank, had bought it specially in Independence for any emergency they might encounter. The few dresses the girls had brought with them were fading and falling apart due to the hot sun beating down on them day after day. The salt from their sweat made the stitching give way.

"There," Rachel declared, "that should hold my dress together for a few more wearings. Are you ready to go to sleep now, Sarah? Me, I'm plumb tuckered out." Sarah Ann nodded, yawned sleepily, and turned out the lamp.

Still yawning early the next morning, Sarah Ann peeped out of the wagon to see what the day was going to be like. Another hot one, she supposed. Reaching for her mirror, she glanced out again to see if anyone else was up yet, then gasped at what she saw! Quietly she reached over and shook Rachel, then put her hand over Rachel's mouth so she couldn't make any sound.

"Sh..sh..sh," she whispered, "be quiet! There are some Indians out there. They're standing near the back of the wagon, so slip out the front and run for Captain Quarles, then get Zeke. Do you understand? Don't make a sound. I'll wake Papa."

Rachel climbed silently down off the wagon seat on the opposite side of the wagon from the Indians, then ran as fast as she could. Moments later she returned to the scene with the Captain and their scout, Zeke. Her father, mother, and a distraught Sarah Ann were standing in their sleeping clothes gaping at the small group of Indians. Sarah still clutched the mirror in her hand. Zeke greeted the scruffy looking Indians in a friendly manner using sign language. He whispered to a group of half-dressed onlookers who were quickly gathering to gawk at the Indians.

"Arapaho! Friendly, let's hope, so smile and act hospitable! Your lives may depend on it!"

The young man was dressed in a buckskin loin cloth and a vest made of cotton. His shiny black hair hung down his back with a clump of hair braided on the side. A headdress of eagle feathers riffled in the breeze. A large bone breastplate covered his hairless chest. His feet were encased in knee-high moccasins wrapped with colorful lacings. Over his left shoulder hung a bow and arrow, and his right hand held a dangerous looking feathered lance. Even though he was partially clothed, he gave the appearance of being nearly naked. Standing proudly beside him was a young mother with her precious baby strapped to her back in a woven bark carrier. Small black eyes looked back warily at anyone brave enough to gawk at the tiny kicking baby. Its mother wore a knee length beaded buckskin dress fringed at the bottom. She wore her long, black hair in two fat braids hanging down her back. Her small feet were encased in beaded moccasins. A strange looking bone necklace hung around her neck.

Slightly behind her stood an old man dressed nearly the same as the young brave. A beaded robe covered his gaunt shoulders. His face was weathered and lined from too many years spent on the plains in all kinds of weather. He was slightly hump-backed and his legs in their knee-high buckskin moccasins were bowed. Squatting on their haunches beside him, a boy about eleven and a girl about seven, sat drawing stick figures in the dirt. Both children were scantily clad, the boy wore buckskin leggings, and the girl wore a buckskin dress similar to her mother's. Using guttural sounds and sign language, it looked like Zeke was having an argument with the Indians. Then he conferred with Captain Quarles. Everyone leaned forward trying to hear what was being said.

"Dag-nab-it! If we give them a steer then we'll have the whole tribe down on us wanting more cattle," the Captain raged at Zeke.

Zeke turned to the crowd and asked, "Kaint you see these hyar folks are just hungry? Just look at how thin those children are. Iffen we don't feed them, it could cause a heap of trouble. They've somehow gotten split up from their tribe. I say let's give them a steer, and some trinkets! Agreed?"

With gestures and the strange guttural sound he made, the young Indian interrupted the argument. Zeke held up his hand to quiet the muttering crowd, "Now he's demanding tobacco, shirts, blankets, food, coffee, and guns, in addition to the beef. You should have agreed to his original demands before he thought to add more to them."

The little group of Indians just stood there and stared at the emigrants while the discussion was being held. Finally everyone agreed on giving the steer to the Indians.

Zeke called out to the drovers in charge of the livestock, "Cut out the worst steer we've got, boys. We sure don't want to give away our best cattle, do we?" All of the Indians and on-lookers went with the drovers to select the steer, but the young Indian woman continued to stand there pointing at Sarah Ann. Trying not to panic, fearful thoughts flitted around in Sarah Ann's head. She was scared stiff.

"Do they mean to take me with them?...why is she looking at me like that?...what does she want?...does she mean me any harm? Oh! I wish I'd never left home!"

Zeke spoke to the determined Indian woman in her language, then turned and relayed the message to Sarah Ann.

"She wants your mirror."

"What? My mirror? But its mine, I've had it since I was eight when Grandma died, and left it especially for me. I won't give it away!" she cried in alarm.

"I reckon you'd better hand it over, she's not leaving without it. An incident like this could bring the whole tribe of thousands down on us. It could be a massacre, honey. Don't think about it, just do it!" Reaching out his hand, Zeke carefully pried Sarah Ann's rigid fingers from the handle, and passed the coveted mirror to the squaw. The Captain had gathered some pretty ribbons and beads from the wagons and offered them to the young Indian woman who greedily gathered them in her arms, then turned to join the departing band. Driving the steer ahead of them, and carrying the heavy bundles of supplies, the band of Indians left the camp without looking back.

Everyone consoled the steer's owner for his loss, and Sarah Ann for her bravery, as they congratulated themselves on still being alive.

6

Soon the gently rolling terrain began to change. The slow moving oxen had pulled the wagons out onto a plateau. The ground they were traveling over was becoming rocky. As they traveled upward, the trail became even steeper. Finally they came to a jump-off point and could go no further. Captain Quarles called a meeting for all the men on the wagon train. As the men stood on the brink of what looked like the edge of the world, they gazed down on a meadow with abundant green grass to feed the livestock. The area they looked upon was Ash Hollow.

But, everyone was asking, "How can we get the wagons down there? It's too steep!" The promontory on which they stood had been named Windlass Hill after a device that was used to raise and lower objects. Everyone listened as Zeke explained plans to get the wagons down.

"I didn't want to frighten you folks travelin' on the train about this difficult part of the trail. We'll have to be cautious and take our time, but come on, men, we can do it!" A cheer rang out and several hats were thrown in the air.

"We'll travel as far down as we can using trees and brush tied to the rear of the wagons to help slow them down. Then we'll hook an extra span of oxen to the back to brake the wagons. We'll have to muscle the wagons down the rest of the way. Stout ropes can be used to swing the wagons over the hardest parts. Then we'll send the women folks and children down the rest of the way with the extra livestock." After such a long speech, Zeke took a minute to stuff a new chaw of tobacco in his mouth. "Who is willing to escort the women?"

"Hey! Horace! How about you going down to Ash Hollow to guard the women?" someone yelled. Horace grinned and nodded his agreement.

Smirking, one man declared, "Or maybe it's the other way around. The women will be guarding Horace!"

As they all laughed and slapped each other on the back, Horace declared, "I never heered such hogwash from you crude fellers! Well, let's quit jawing and get the job done!"

Contents of the wagons were tied on any livestock they thought could carry it in order to lighten the wagons. Trees and brush were cut down and stacked nearby. Crews were selected for each job. Drivers were chosen for their strength and dependability. Women and children herding the heavily loaded animals had gone ahead accompanied by Horace and a few others who would be little use in the difficult task ahead. Their assignment was to set up camp down below in Ash Hollow, and be prepared for any medical emergencies that might come up.

One crew chained trees and brush to the back of the wagon, while another crew hooked a span of oxen at the rear to brace and hold it back. If the wagon went too fast it would overrun the oxen in the front and go crashing down the mountain, destroying the wagon and killing the oxen. The driver would inch down the descent with his brake on as slowly as he could, trying his best to keep control.

Another crew waited to lever the wagon down further by rope. Hour after hour the men labored. Freak accidents happened. A wheel on one of the wagons came off sending the oxen, wagon, and all its contents hurtling off into space. Fortunately, the driver jumped in time to save his life but suffered a broken leg. Everyone was distressed at the loss of two yoke of valuable oxen, but happy the driver survived. One of the rope handlers caught a finger in the rope and it was severely mangled. An ox fell in the harness, was dragged and had to be destroyed. It took two long weary days to lever the wagons down into luxurious Ash Hollow. Then, two more days to get the caravan into readiness for the dreary routine of the trail, again.

Folks agreed that Windlass Hill was an appropriate name for that perpendicular hill which had caused so many problems for the wagon train. Happy at the successful results of their descent, a party was held with food, music, and dancing. A few luckless chickens, who swayed in crates at the rear of many wagons, were sacrificed to the cooking pot for the celebration. Black iron kettles hanging on pot hooks over campfires, contained delicious chicken and dumplings for the festivities that evening. Emigrants grown gaunt from the lack of sufficient food along the devastating trail, rubbed their empty stomachs in anticipation of the feast. Everyone got some rest, did their necessary chores, then had a good time at the party.

Before supper, Horace washed his face, combed his hair, put on a clean shirt, then picked some wild flowers for Cordelia. Needing courage he took a little nip from the flask he carried in his hip pocket. He advanced on her just as she set the pot of chicken and dumplings on the make-shift table. Turning, she saw him standing there with a red face holding the flowers out to her.

"These here fl..owers are for y..ou, Cordelia!" Horace groaned to himself at the sound of his voice cracking. He had meant to sound dignified.

"What's all this fol-der-al?" Cordelia snorted. "I don't hold with fripperies!"

59

"I figured you and me ought to get hitched seeing as you ain't got nobody but Samson to take care of you." Horace blurted out recklessly.

"Hitched?" squealed Cordelia. "You must be funnin' me, Horace."

"Cross my heart, hope to die...if I don't tell the truth...may yore cat spit in my eye!"

"Horace, you can't be serious! I surely do appreciate the help you been givin' me by drivin' the wagon and all, but marriage. Ha!" Shaking her head, Cordelia bent over in laughter at the solemn look on Horace's face. Frowning, she sniffed his breath, "Why, you little rat-tailed varmint! Is that liquor I smell on your breath?"

"You are the most pig-headed woman I ever did see. Why I was fool enough to think we could ever set horses, is beyond me. Just forget I mentioned it. But, remember, 'Once burned, twice shy!' Think on it!" Trying to hold onto his pride, Horace stalked away.

Samson stretched lazily, then curled himself around Cordelia's feet, as she watched Horace walk away with his shoulders slumped. "There goes a real lonesome man, Samson. Maybe I just might think on it!" she mumbled.

"Me..ow!

Thanks to Zeke's good advice, the dysentery that had threatened the health of the pioneers was under control. After several days of travel in white alkaline dust that caused their eyes to be red and sore from the grit, a gigantic rock resembling a courthouse came into view in the distance. Zeke had been scouting far ahead of the wagon train. As he waited for the train to catch up, sitting relaxed on his pinto, he stuffed a fresh chaw of tobacco in his mouth. Wagon drivers halted their wagons as they gazed at the view. After days of looking at nothing except rolling knolls on the prairie, their eyes feasted on the site. Several young people left their wagons and clustered around Zeke to ask questions.

Zeke drawled, "It's called Courthouse Rock, because it looks just like a big round courthouse. I reckon its about 200 feet high. Mostly lime rock from an old volcano. They call that little rock yonder, Jail House Rock cause it sorta stands guard. When we get closer you'll see the Post Office ledge where folks leave messages for the emigrants that follow. The ledge is full of water worn rock fissures, caused from years of rainwater. Some folks wrote on bleached buffalo skulls or left written notes tucked into crevices. Someone cut the words 'POST OFFICE' into the rock. When we make camp later today, you young'uns can climb up on top of Courthouse Rock and carve your names in the rock. I reckon you'd like that. Now, let's get this hyar train moving!"

The younger folks, and those with determination, climbed the rock before sundown to scratch their names in the sandstone. They read other names, many were well known, before carefully climbing down the rock in time for supper.

After they had eaten, Zeke told tales around the campfire. He related an interesting legend about the strange rock formation. The group was completely spellbound as he told about a small party of Pawnee Indians camped near the rock who had been surprised by a war party of Sioux Indians. The Pawnee climbed up the rock for safety. The crafty Sioux waited at the bottom for the trapped party of Pawnee to come down and surrender, or starve on top of the barren rock. Suffering from lack of food and water, the cornered Pawnee despaired after two days had passed. When darkness fell again, their Chief prayed in desperation to his God for guidance, and received instructions for escape. At daybreak, he searched and found a cleft in the rock. That night, under cover of darkness, the clever Pawnee tied all their lariats together, stampeded their horses down the trail to distract the Sioux war party, then slid down their rope ladder and made their escape.

"OK, that's enough stories for tonight. Let's all hit the hay, we'll get an early start tomorrow," Zeke announced as he rolled to his feet and sauntered off toward his bedroll.

In a haze off in the distance, the landmark Chimney Rock could barely be seen. Zeke had warned that this area was prone to electrical storms, and previous wagon trains had encountered roving bands of Indians. Zeke declared he would double the guard, as they approached Chimney Rock. Well over 100 feet high, Chimney Rock had a tall cone of red sandstone rising in a lofty spire that stood on top of the rock, and..."Looms like a beckoning finger to encourage the traveler." This appendage was over 40 feet high. It could be seen nearly 50 miles away. Many of the plains Indians named it the "Tepee" because it resembled their nomadic homes made out of hides and sticks.

As they drew closer to Chimney Rock, near sunset, some of the horsemen riding out in front to help select a campsite were startled by a man stepping out from behind some brush. The horses reared and whinnied their distress, unseating one unwary rider.

At first the men thought the intruder was an Indian. He had long straggly black hair, pulled back by a head band, fringed buckskin shirt and leggings, beaded knee-high moccasins and tattered red long johns peeking out from under his shirt. Spotted with grease, the frontier clothes looked well used. A nearly flattened, well worn hat, hung by a rawhide string down his back. Carelessly thrown over his shoulder was a tarnished double barreled ten gauge sawed-off shotgun. Hanging on his left hip, along with some bags fashioned from deerskin, was a huge shiny knife, gleaming as the sun flashed from its surface. Slung low on his right hip, a revolver hung nestled in a well worn holster. All eyes looked at the stranger warily as his left hand stroked the handle of the knife. On his chest dangled a necklace with one gleaming bear tooth. A long whittled toothpick hung from the corner of his mouth.

From a distance Samuel observed the fellow standing in full view. Obviously a man of great experience on the frontier. Not a young man for his slightly slumped posture and the many wrinkles around his eyes betrayed his advancing age.

Samuel narrowed his eyes and gave a little whistle as he mumbled to himself, "Dan..ger..ous!"

Samuel rode closer, his horse sliding to a halt in front of the stranger. As they stared at each other in surprise, a vigilant hawk lazily circled overhead searching for a meal.

"Well, I do declare!" exclaimed Samuel "who might you be, mister?" His fingers itched to reach for his gun. "We're with that wagon train yonder."

"Howdy do, folks!" the stranger drawled. "I'm Jedediah Simmons, most recent from out West. Been doin' a mite prospecting, a tad buffalo skinning, and some lollygagging around this fine country hyar." As he talked he reached up a dirty finger and rubbed his neck under the scratchy long johns. "I used to be a fur trader out in the Oregon Territory before those dad-burned English killed all them there beaver. Put me diddly-squat right out of business, they did." Pulling cigarette fixings out of his pocket he squatted on his haunches and began to roll a smoke.

Leaning from his saddle, Samuel stretched out his hand and said, "Glad to make your acquaintance. Samuel Elliott at your service. My wife and two sons are waiting over yonder with that there wagon train. What in tarnation are you doin' way out hyar without a horse? Seems to me a durn-fool thing to do?" Samuel declared, as he gestured at the wide open spaces with his hand.

"Oh, I got me a horse alright, don't you worry yourself none on my account. A smart fella gets the lay of the land before he reveals everythin' about his business. Yessiree! I'm a smart fella, you bettcha! Looks just like we all gonna be friends."

A loud whistle startled the men on horseback causing their horses to snort and dance. From the concealment of the brush a scruffy looking sorrel mare with white mane and tail, cantered out answering the whistle. Her eyes were wild-looking and her empty stirrups bounced as she moved. A bed roll and several packs were tied behind a well worn saddle.

"Over hyar, sweet thing," the stranger called as he waved his hat. The mare flattened her ears, and flared her nostrils as she slid to a stop in front of Jedediah, her big white teeth snapping at the other horses.

"Watch out!" one of the men called out while he backed his horse out of the way, "That there mare is a mean one."

"Naw, she ain't," chuckled Jedediah, "that's just her way. She thinks she's protecting me. She don't like nobody else, and that's a fact!" Slapping his hat on his knee, he joked with a wide grin, "Y'all need to keep an eye on yore children, cuz that there ornery critter will eat anything. She nibbles on rawhide, wood, hair, fingers, anythin' a'tall! She just ain't particular like, but best give her lots of room, 'cause she can be a mite nasty, sometimes. She's bad-tempered, kicks worse than a mule, but Darlin's sure-footed as a cat, and the old fool thinks she's my wife!" he declared, patting her nose as she slobbered and whiffled at his hand. "Now Darlin' behave yourself, these hyar are nice folks."

Samuel chuckled to himself, tipped his hat back on his head, as he watched Jedediah mount up. "Why don't you and Darlin' there join up with our wagon train? We're on our way out to Oregon. We can always use another gun hand. Looks like you know how to handle yourself in a gunfight."

"I do declare, y'all got Oregon Fever. But, I reckon that's as good an idea as any. Darlin' and me will have a little chat about it. She usually knows what's best. Until then I could use a good meal."

The men rode back to the campsite to the smell of bacon sizzling and biscuits browning. Jed's mouth watered at the tantalizing smells. His nose twitched at the aroma of coffee perking over an open fire as he approached the camp. His provisions had long ago run out, and he was living on pemmican some Indians had given him, and some coffee made from boiled parched wheat. The horsemen rode up and dismounted with the newcomer in the group. Women and children approached with caution when the stranger was noticed. As Samuel introduced him to the crowd, a big crooked smile lighted Jedediah's wrinkled face. That smile broke the ice and everyone made him feel welcome.

All the campers, including Darlin' and Jedediah, were ready the next morning as they listened to the Captain's call, "We've got a lot of ground to cover. Let's roll!"

Each person stared at Chimney Rock with its beckoning finger as the wagon train slowly passed by. The plodding obedient oxen walked approximately 2 miles per hour, sometimes making the emigrants wish they were using mules. Then they had to remind themselves many people could not get across the vast mountains with mules that were not as strong as oxen. Each delay made their chances slimmer of reaching their destination before the winter snows made the mountains impassable. Every day, they pushed their reluctant bodies into forward motion. After last night's merriment, Jedediah finished telling his hilarious stories, and declared that all his new friends were to call him Jed.

7

As the wagon train wended its way slowly over the rolling prairie, Jed came riding up to the Brandon wagon. Tipping his hat politely to Rebeccah he asked, "Ma'am, Darlin' hyar would just love to have little Rachel come ridin' with us this mornin', iffen you please. I ain't got no family left, and I dearly love little children."

"I'm worried about that horse. She looks very wicked to me," declared Rebeccah, keeping a wary eye on Darlin'.

"Well now, she promised she wouldn't do no acting up this hyar morning," Jed vowed as he patted Darlin's neck.

Rachel was bouncing on the wagon seat eager to ride the horse. No one had any time to give a little girl a ride. With a beseeching look at her mother she wailed, "Oh please, Ma! Can't I go, pl..e.e.e.se?"

"I guess so, this time. But don't be gone long," Becky agreed, with some concern showing in her eyes. Soon Rachel was settled on the saddle in front of Jed.

"See those bluffs off yonder in the distance? Just a few miles north of Chimney Rock stands another Oregon Trail landmark called Scott's Bluff in the Nebraska badlands. Around the camp-fires at night, old frontiersmen like Jim Bridger, Jed Smith, Joe

Walker and Benjamin Bonneville, and me, love to tell how that there bluff got its name. About 1828, a party of fur hunters were traveling down the river when their canoes overturned. The water ruined their powder so they couldn't hunt for food. They dug roots from the frozen ground and ate some wild berries to keep from starvin'. Hiram Scott, a rugged mountaineer got too sick to travel. Afraid that if they lingered until he died they would all perish, the hunters abandoned Scott. By abandoning Scott to his fate, they felt they would have a chance to catch up to a party reported to be on the trail ahead. After all, he would soon die, why should they lose their only hope of rescue. They did catch up with the huntin' party but concealed their abandonment of Scott. Another huntin' party stumbled upon Scott's bleached bones the followin' summer which were identified by his papers and clothes. His remains were found sixty miles from where the legend says Scott was left to die. The determined man had crawled until he met his death. There ain't much a rugged frontiersman kaint do. That's some story, huh? Folks say that's how that series of cliffs got named Scott's Bluff."

"Aw, Jed, are you fooling me?" Rachel asked with a huge grin on her face.

"Child, I hope to die, iffin it ain't the truth!"

"Jed, May I ask you a question?"

"Shoot, yes! Ask away, child."

"How come you to go way out West and become a scout?"

"Dumplin' yore treadin' on some tender memories there. My Ma and Pa died with smallpox back in 1816 when I was just fourteen years old. Some over zealous neighbors afraid of catching the pox, set our old house on fire. Well, the fire jumped to the barns and sheds killin' the animals, but one old burro that was tied out under a tree. Two little precious sisters and my onliest brother, died in the fire. The only reason I survived was

I was fishin' down at the creek. I was pure flummoxed as to what to do next. I stayed near the fire all night to keep warm. The next mornin' I cried out all my tears, blew my nose, got on that burro and took off out West to look for my fortune. I might add, I ain't found it yet!" Jed chuckled.

"I'm real sorry, Jed," Rachel whispered as she wiped a tear from her eye.

"Hey, that was a long, long time ago. I've all but forgot it. You forget it too, honey. Old Jed's doin' just fine!"

"What does a scout do?" Blowing her nose on Jed's old handkerchief, Rachel changed to a different subject.

"I reckon he guides folks who don't know which end of a horse bites and which end kicks, wherever they want to go. You see child, folks like me just keep on wanderin'. We been over every mountain, crossed every stream from the Atlantic Ocean to the Pacific Ocean. I reckon I tried to eat all the dust in this hyar country. You eat it in your food, sleep with it, wear it on your clothes, and in the winter it sticks to you like glue." Jed slapped Darlin's head away as she turned her head and tried to nip at his knee. "Kaint you see I'm talking to this hyar child? You see, honey," he continued, "mountainmen carry a bit of beans, salt pork, flour and a pinch of coffee in their packs. When that's all gone we live off the land. After a while you just have a sixth sense of where you are. Most of the time I watch for landmarks like Chimney Rock or Independence Rock to guide me. Certain trees, the shape of a mountain, the color of the river, rock formations, all are stored in your memory. By day, you watch the sun, by night you use the stars to guide you. I reckon I've sat around more campfires than I can count. After I eat my meal, I wipe my greasy fingers on my buckskins, because the grease helps keep the cold wind out. Anymore questions, dumplin'?"

He looked down at Rachel's nodding head. Grinning, he headed Darlin' back to the wagon train. The little sweetheart was asleep!

Early next morning a hunting party was getting ready to set out from camp. This time some of the younger boys were allowed to participate so they could learn the responsibility of hunting. Jonathan was allowed to join in the hunt, since Zeke and Jed would be there to help teach the younger ones. Samuel volunteered to drive the wagon, so his son could get in some much needed hunting practice. Sarah Ann was visiting with an excited Jonathan while he prepared his gear, and tied it on his father's fidgety horse. As he was getting ready to mount and say goodbye to Sarah, he heard a loud "Boom" nearby. Dropping the reins, he was already running in the direction the sound had come. He called back to Sarah Ann, "Somebody's probably shooting at a snake. I'll be right back. Stay right there and keep an eye on Pa's horse," he ordered.

As Jonathan ran he was thinking to himself, "Indians." He was glad he had grabbed his old shotgun. A large crowd was gathering near one of the wagons. His brother Benjamin joined him as he ran. They tried to get up close to the crowd where they could see what was going on. One of Jonathan's friends lay on the ground, with blood all over his chest. His face was as white as a sheet.

"What happened?" Jonathan asked excitedly! "Who shot him? Indians?"

"Calm down, boy," Jed answered soothingly, "he shot his own self. Any fool can see it was an accident. He was draggin' the rifle out of the wagon...got careless...it caught on somethin'...and Blam!"

At last the doctor was there and was putting the young injured man on a make-shift stretcher.

"He ain't dead, just unconscious. Doc'll help him if anyone can." Jed tried to console Jonathan who was almost in tears.

"Let's mount up boys, you can't help him none, and we've got meat to git today," Zeke called as he swung up onto his saddle.

The downcast party of young hunters rode out of camp reluctantly, looking back as if they expected their wounded friend to join them.

Later in the afternoon, a thunder storm brought them back quickly. Everyone had been too upset to keep their minds on hunting game. Several days later, the unfortunate boy died. The rifle ball had lodged near the backbone, and he had lost too much blood to live. Doc had tried his best but couldn't save him. Some of the men made a crude wooden coffin and buried him on the trail. No rocks could be found to build a cairn, so to protect it from predators the wagons ran over the grave to disguise it. The family and all his friends on the wagon train were devastated but they must continue their journey. Each day, time was their enemy, and they were beginning to realize how precious it was. They had already been on the trail much too long. The speed of their traveling time, must increase.

As a brilliant dawn spread its red and gold fingers across the dark sky, Zeke and Jed stood gazing in a northerly direction, sniffing at the early morning breeze. Zeke shaded his eyes from the fast approaching sun with his hand.

"Yep, I was a-feared that's what I smelled," Jed said quietly as he finished cutting his last fingernail, closed the knife and dropped it back into his pocket.

"Prairie fire!" exclaimed Zeke. "What you reckon we ought to do?"

"Well...iffen yore asking...I highly recommend we make a run for it with our tails tucked up behind us."

"I agree. Let's tell the others." They broke camp rapidly under Zeke's orders to be "quick about it. No lollygagging!"

Whips cracked, leather creaked, cattle lowed, pigs squealed, chains rattled, as the wagon train raced to get out of the path of the smoldering fire. Soon the crackling of the fire and the pounding of the animal's hooves broke the silence of the prairie. They saw an occasional deer, prairie dog, or rabbit running away from the heat. Grouse and partridge ran across the grass covered plains then took to the air in fearful flight as the flames grew closer.

"Faster!" urged the two scouts, pushing their lathered horses to the limits.

"Come on, folks, we're going to make it!"

Some of the wooden wheels caught fire. Women and children quickly dipped water from the barrels, and sloshed it over the sides of the wagons, down over the smoking wheels. Most of the terrified animals ran ahead of the slower wagons. It was unbearably hot. Wide horrified eyes stared at the orange flames licking at the wagons. Smoke filled the air and stole their breaths.

Captain Quarles called encouragement, "Just a little further to the edge of the fire and it will miss us."

As the wagons neared the edge where the fire would bypass them, one of the slower wagons bringing up the rear, overturned, breaking an axle directly in the path of the fire. The contents of the wagon spilled out on the ground as it overturned. Astonished breaths held as they watched, then were expelled as the unlucky occupants crawled up on the broken wagon. The roaring fire swept close, as bright orange flames licked at the wood.

"Reckon me and Darlin' better go fetch those folks while there's still time," Jed drawled as he stuck one foot in the stirrup.

"Nobody can save them now, it's too dangerous!" Horace shouted.

Zeke's hand closed over Jed's arm as he was about to swing up onto his saddle. "Wait a minute, Jed. Darlin's not shod. You can't risk her like that. She's like family to you. My horse is wearing iron horseshoes that will shed some of the heat from the fire. Don't give me any guff cause I'm going after those folks!"

As he spoke, Zeke leaped over the back of his horse in a daring mount, landed in the saddle, kicked his horse into a dead run and was halfway to the shrieking family in the midst of the fire, before the folks on the wagon train were aware of what was happening. All too glad of the rescue, the family climbed on, or hung on the side of the horse as Zeke turned him back toward safety.

As the rapidly moving horse approached, three cheers rang out in honor of Zeke's bravery.

"Hip, hip, hooray! Hip, hip, hooray! Hip, hip, hooray!"

The family thanked Zeke with grateful tears, as they patted Zeke's pinto pony and poured water on the scorched hair around his smoking hooves. Everyone was jubilant over the close call of the fire trapped family and their astounding rescue. Sparks blown on the wind had done considerable damage to hair and clothes. To relieve the tension, everyone was laughing at the sight of the animals with scorched hair, and the burned holes in clothing worn by the emigrants. Soon, the expected shout came down the line. "Let's roll!"

Day after weary day they, walked or rode, mile after mile, through sagebrush, sand, mud, up and down hills, and across raging rivers. It seemed to rain nearly every day making the trail a sea of mud. The next day everything was dry and dusty again, and the wagon wheels scraped deep ruts in the land. It seemed the thirsty land drank the rainwater.

One day excitement swirled through the wagon train. Fort Laramie was in sight. Imagine the delight at the first sight of the fort. Civilization at last! At first, all they could see was a fifteen foot wall enclosing the remote fort. As they drew nearer they observed warehouses for storing goods. A fur trading shelter stood in the middle of the square. Some rundown shops and houses for workers and travelers completed the tiny fort. A wooden partition wall formed a corral for fort animals. The crumbling adobe buildings were in poor repair.

Bewhiskered trappers, unkempt traders, curious Indians, and noisy children bustled around the fort gawking at the newcomers. After pulling the wagons as close to the fort as they could, the weary emigrants rested and rejoiced as they set up a temporary camp. Now in Wyoming Territory, they were one step closer to their final goal. Their destination...the Willamette Valley...land of milk and honey...was becoming a reality. Celebrations were held at the campfires that night. The day had been spent making needed repairs and stocking up with the few supplies that were left at the tiny fort. Earlier trains had depleted many of the supplies. Heavy wagon wheels being repaired brought incessant hammering and banging from the blacksmith's shed. Travel weary horses had to be reshod.

Banjoes, fiddles, harmonicas and stomping feet replaced the ringing blacksmith's sounds that evening, after all the chores were done. Everyone was dancing, even the children.

Sarah Ann ran to her wagon calling to her mother, "Ma, they're fixing to announce the handkerchief dance. May I dance it just this once?"

"But, Sarah Ann, you know that's a courting dance, don't you?"

"Of course I know, Ma. But, I'm fourteen now, and some of the other girls are going to dance. Will you let me?" she asked, while her face wore a serious expression.

"Alright, honey. Here's my best handkerchief. Run on, now, and have a good time."

With a shout of delight, Sarah ran back to the campfire to join the dancing. They were calling for one more girl to even the numbers, as she ran up. The men were already circled in the middle with their backs to the girls. The girls began to promenade around the men, giggling as they danced. As they selected their dance partner, they dropped the handkerchief behind him and continued to dance around the circle until all the girls had selected their partner and had stopped behind him. They took two steps out and turned their backs. The men then turned around, bent down, picked up the handkerchief, and tapped the girl on the shoulder. When she turned to face him, he handed the handkerchief to her, then made a deep bow. She then, gave him a curtsey, and they began the courting dance.

Jed had declared causing much laughter, "that he would dance with all the ladies, Darlin' included."

Jed and Rachel were dancing a reel until Jed declared he was "plumb tuckered out." Rachel collapsed on a box while Jed squatted on the ground, took out the makings and began to roll a smoke as they gazed at the flickering firelight.

"I didn't know you could dance a jig like that, Jed," Rachel mentioned as she wiped her perspiring face.

"Oh, shucks! I was just showing off! I shouldn't have tried doin' a buck and wing at my age. I'll have to leave that for those younger fellas. This hyar old heart almost gave out on me and I thought I was ready to meet my maker."

As they sat resting quietly watching busy fireflies flicker in the night, Jed said as he licked the edge of the paper to seal it, "You look mighty thoughtful, tonight, honey. Penny for your thoughts?"

"I was kind of scared back at the prairie fire. Aren't you scared of anything, Jed," Rachel asked?

"Me? Why sure. There's two things I'm a-feared of."

"What are those two things your scared of, Jed?"

"I'm scared of hearin' those iron doors slam on the calaboose."

"What in thunderation is a cal...a...boose?" Rachel, realizing what she had said, covered her mouth in dismay to keep from giggling.

"Please don't tell Ma I used *THAT* word, Jed. One day I overheard Pa saying 'thunderation' and Ma said she had a good mind to wash his mouth out with soap."

"Don't worry yore pretty little head about that. I wouldn't say nothin' to get you in trouble with yore Ma," Jed declared.

"Back in my younger years, I wandered down into Mexican Territory and cut up a little. The judge threatened to throw me in the Calabozo, that there is Mexican for jail. Well sir, I got me a good look into that filthy jail, and it wasn't a place I wanted to spend any time. I thought I was gonna faint when the judge said, 'Git out of Mexican Territory! And don't ever come back!' Boy howdy, I lit out of that town faster than greased lightening!"

"And the other thing you're scared of, Jed?"

"Well, I confess, I'm a-feared of bein' 'launched into eternity'!"

"What does that mean? That sounds silly!"

"It means I'm scared of bein' hung, that's what," chuckling, Jed winked an eye at Rachel.

"Aren't you scared of Indians? I sure am."

As Jed smoked, he blew smoke rings for Rachel to poke her finger through as they gazed lazily at the stars glittering against a dark sky.

"You don't need to be scared here at the fort. Most of these Indians are Dakotas, Utes, Paiutes, Diggers and Pawnees. Some of them have been to Mission Schools and can speak at least some English. They are pretty tame compared to the ones out on the plains. Those Indians attack the travelers, run off livestock, steal horses, ambush stragglers, and cause mischief. We'll soon be going through Cheyenne and Sioux lands, they're fierce warriors who often seize captives, and take 'coup.'(coo) To an Indian, takin' coup means anythin' from scalping, to touchin' his opponent. It's a matter of pride to an Indian. They are just tryin' to protect their lands from the White man's encroachment. They believe that 'Mother Earth' is sacred and provides everythin' they need to survive. Plains Indians believe in animal powers, the strength of the buffalo, the speed of the antelope, and the bravery of the eagle. Many Indians are not happy with the Whites coming onto their lands. The chief of the Ogalala Sioux, Red Cloud, likened the number of Whites intrudin' on Indian tribal lands to 'blades of grass in the Spring!' But not to worry, we've got plenty of firepower to protect you."

"Rachel, honey, it's time for you to get tucked up in your bed. We gettin' a mighty early start in the mornin'. Darlin's waitin' for me to come scratch her ears and tuck her in for the night."

"Why do you call your horse, Darling?" giggled Rachel, "That's a silly name for a horse."

"I gave up on women a long time ago. Then maybe it's the other way around. Maybe they gave up on me," Jed declared, as he chuckled and stomped on his cigarette with his scuffed boot. "I kaint sit around no parlor drinkin' tea and crookin' my little finger to please some dad-blamed female. They won't have nothin' to do with ya iffen ya ain't civilized. My mare understands me like no woman ever could. We been through drought, prairie fires, starvation, and Indian attacks." Jed declared, with pride for his horse shining in his eyes.

"I'll tell you a little story before you run off to bed. One day she outran a parcel of mighty mean looking braves painted up for war. They was lookin' down our necks when she swiveled to the left and took off hell-bent for leather down a draw. A-fore they could get their horses turned around to chase us, she had crossed a creek and was hidden in some trees. I just sat on that saddle and held on for dear life. I told myself, I reckon Darlin' knows what she's doin'. She's cantankerous, mean and ornery, not to mention opinionated but she looks after me better'n any wife ever could. That's why I call her Darlin'. Ya better get to bed, Rachel honey, I hear your Ma a-callin'. See ya in the mornin'."

8

Heavy rains awakened the company the next day. Rachel looked out at the dark sky and missed seeing the glorious red, gold, pink and mauve sunrise. Thunder rumbled across the sky and lightning danced far off in the distance. Those that had leftover food from the day before were fortunate because no breakfast was cooked that day. Everyone else went hungry.

As the oxen plodded along in the mud, Jed rode Darlin' alongside the slow moving wagon and told Rachel about the Red Bluff area they were passing through. He seemed to be worried about something. A frown replaced his usual lopsided grin. As was customary, his fingers searched for an itch under his tattered long johns.

"What's bothering you, Jed? Even Darlin's wearing a frown this morning." as Rachel spoke, she pulled her braid out of Darlin's mouth, tucked it up under her bonnet, and tapped his nose in warning.

"I reckon I'm studyin' about the river crossin'. That there North Platte is swole up pretty good from the rain we had last night. Just makes me a mite worried. Darlin' thinks I need to jaw with Zeke and the Captain. See ya later, sugar." Darlin' did a little dance, then settled down into a slow canter, as Jed tipped his hat to Rachel and rode off looking for the Captain.

After the rain stopped, the sweltering heat returned. It was suffocating, making it difficult to breathe. With each step the white alkali dust swirled over everything. The blistering wind never seemed to rest in its ceaseless blowing over the landscape littered with whitened animal carcasses. Soon the river came in sight.

It was indeed swollen and the current was as "rapid as a millrace." At least 80 yards wide, the sight of its murky water was forbidding. Debris swirled around in eddies as it raced along.

The Captain, Zeke, and Samuel rode their horses side by side across the river. The three spread out so their path through the water was as wide as a wagon. In this way, they could check the depth of the water and the condition of the bottom. While they were across the river, they anchored a huge towline rope to the bank. Safely back across, Captain Quarles called out to the company, "Quickly, men, unpack your wagons and use anything you can to raise the wagon bed up a foot at least, more if you can. I saw some buffalo skulls down the trail aways. They'll do just fine. Empty a box or two, or maybe a bucket. Let's get in a hustle men, we're wasting daylight."

The unloading was done in quick order. Wagon beds were braced up as high as they could with old skulls or empty boxes. After being reloaded, the first wagons were ready to begin to ford the river with its ugly currents. With a loop around the towline rope anchor, and a rope tied to the saddle of a horse on each side, the occupants felt fairly secure making the crossing. Most of the crossing was routine, until one wagon swerved to avoid a limb coming swiftly down river, directly in the path of the oxen. Bawling loudly, the frightened animals attempted to turn in the water and return to the bank, spinning the prairie schooner into the hazardous current. Seeing the danger, the wagon occupants dived in the water and began swimming to shore, in an attempt to save themselves. Riders quickly sailed ropes over their heads for them to grab in an attempt to save their lives.

Knowing the wagon could not be saved, the two out-riders cut the restraining ropes before the weight pulled them under. One managed to unhook the oxen just as the anchored rope gave way. The oxen righted themselves and wallowed to the far bank. The rest of the company, from both banks, watched the wagon tumble and break up in the raging water, thinking how lucky they were they had only lost one wagon. The unfortunate family was absorbed into the train and was given a helping hand to Oregon.

The next stop, Willow Springs, made an ideal camping spot. Everyone was glad to rest in such a pleasant spot with its shade and green grass and plenty of water. They hated to leave, but after a day of unscheduled rest they felt ready to resume the trip. Next stop would be Independence Rock.

Half blinded by the glaring sun, their bloodshot eyes feasted on the sight of Independence Rock on the Sweetwater River. A landmark on the Oregon Trail, the "Great Record of the Desert," has many names inscribed on the sandstone rock. It resembles a huge turtle sprawled in the desert among the prickly cactus and sagebrush. The rock, nearly 200 feet high in places was nearly flat on top.

The slow progress of the wagon train halted many times as sharp rocks, cactus spines, and grass stubble cut and bruised the emigrant's feet, and the hooves of the suffering livestock. To prevent further damage to the oxen's hooves, campfires were built to heat tar to be applied to their hooves. Sometimes it was necessary to tie pieces of canvas around their hooves to protect them from the rough travel.

Rachel and Sarah Ann sewed tiny little boots for Quincy. He rode in the wagon most of the time now, for he tired easily. Wagons broke down and wheels had to be repaired. Herds of buffalo were sighted in the distance. The barely visible trail was becoming steep and stony.

The trail now left the familiar Platte River to follow the Sweetwater. It needed no other name since the rugged mountaineers claimed that to go out West and cross the Sweetwater proved your worth and made you a "real man!" Around the campfires at night they told how the Sweetwater got its name, swearing "to the truth of the story!"

This legend has been repeated many times over the years: A weary troop of fur traders on their return trip from Fort Bridger, after trading their winter furs, attempted to cross a swollen river. Mules carrying heavy winter supplies, reluctant to enter the frigid fast-moving water, acted up. The fur traders forced the reluctant mules into the river provoking one to buck. His frantic bucking caused a 100 pound sack of sugar to fall into the river, melting immediately.

One of the trappers declared, "Well! Ah'll be a freckle-faced toad! Don't that beat all! That there is the sweetest water I ever did see!" Every since, the infamous river has been called the Sweetwater.

While camped near a wedged shaped fissure with turbulent water splashing through located on the Sweetwater River, called Devil's Gate, a small hunting party from the wagon train went out to scour the countryside for game. Several miles away and out of sight of the train, they suddenly became surrounded by a hunting party of Sioux Indians. Pointing sharp feathered lances at the frightened men, they indicated they wanted them to ride toward a nearby knoll. Fearing they would be killed, they obeyed and rode in that direction. Returning from scouting the area, Zeke was just in time to observe the horsemen disappear over the small hill. Riding as fast as his tired horse could carry him, he overtook the wagon train shouting as he approached.

"Halloo there! Men! Mount up with all the firepower you can carry. You women, gather up all the trade goods you can find in a hurry. Hustle now, so we can rescue your loved ones from the Indians!" As his horse slid to a halt, the company was already jumping to his orders. Questions were hurled at him from all directions.

"I don't have time to answer questions now. Someone get me a fresh horse, mine's done in. Make sure it's a fast one. You men there, guard the train, and look sharp, this could be a trap!"

Throwing his saddle over the fresh mount, he called, "Follow me, men!"

They raced their horses toward the knoll at breakneck speed. Zeke prayed that the few minutes wasted getting the men mounted and ready to go had not meant the captives were already dead. He motioned for one group, with Jed as leader, to circle the knoll and rush in at a signal while he led his group from the opposite side. Hoping that surprise would save the captive men, they came at full speed at the Indians who were busy tying the struggling men on their horses. They had stripped off all their clothes and had taken their firearms. The Indians felt the act of stripping the clothes off their captives humiliated them and deprived them of their power. Zeke and Jed dismounted while the rest of the group held their guns on the straggly band of Sioux. Speaking in a guttural tongue and using sign language the two experienced scouts managed to trade for the hostages. Eagerly, the Indians traded for five twists of tobacco for each man and a handful of Indian trinkets. With fierce scowls on their faces, the Indians mounted their ponies and rode away. After pulling on their boots and donning their clothes the still shaking captives and their rescuers rode back to the wagon train. Smug grins of relief on their faces betrayed how grateful they felt at the promptness of their rescue.

Continuing on with their journey, the emigrants feared the worst was still to come for they were ascending into the Great Rocky Mountains. This beautiful terrain, with rugged bluffs and rolling hills, was called high plains country. Instead of the burning heat, they often had high winds to contend with. Now everything had to be tied to the wagon so it wouldn't blow away. One wagon was caught crosswise to the wailing wind and was blown over, spilling its contents. Flour, beans, and coffee were strewn over the side of the mountain. Much of their family's precious food could not be salvaged and had to be discarded.

Before leaving the river behind, each wagon had to soak their wooden wheels. If the wood became too dry it would shrink away from the metal rims causing problems with the wheel. Everyone made sure the barrels were full and they were carrying as much water as the barrels would hold. Dry fuel for cooking fires was scarce. Constant wearing, with little washing, was causing clothes to wear out much too soon. Patch was sewed on top of patch.

The hunters could find little game. At Fort Laramie, some friendly Indians had shown them how to dry buffalo strips over the fire. Even though they disliked the taste, they had followed the advice and dried the tough stringy meat. Again, nearly starving they struggled upwards, surprised at the gradual ascent. Rest stops became more frequent.

Husbands demanded wives throw out some of their cherished possessions to help lighten the load. Bed frames, bureaus, sewing machines, and even stoves were discarded. Emotional tears ran down the women's sun ravaged dirty faces, as they watched the men pitch out the heavier items. The ground was already littered with items thrown away by preceding wagon trains.

Sometimes an extra yoke of oxen had to be attached to get some heavier wagons farther along the steep trail. Several times, the Elliott's heavy Conestoga wagon needed additional help. Many felt strangely light-headed due to the higher elevation. Keening cries of eagles were heard overhead. Often, the yip and howl of coyotes could be heard in the distance. Pure mountain air made the distant animals sound closer than they were. An occasional fir tree, spruce, or aspen appeared to be stunted from the high altitude and the frigid winters. Sometimes, if the day was clear, a gleaming alabaster peak could be seen in the distance.

One day a rider came racing into camp slapping his battered hat against his leg, yelling, "We're across the Continental Divide! Hallelujah!" he whooped hoarsely. "Crossing South Pass wasn't so hard." Shouting loudly to anyone who would listen, he joined the jubilant company who were also cheering in happiness. He related how he had observed the streams were now flowing west instead of flowing east. Jed had told them all to watch for westward flowing streams.

Dazzling lakes off in the distance looked like liquid emeralds. Eager creeks rushed down steep ravines, as if they couldn't wait to get to the bottom of the mountain. Delicate white clouds, reminding one of frosting on a cake, floated lazily across the cobalt blue sky. Weary emigrants rejoiced just to be alive on such a delightful day.

Descending from the mountains was not an easy task. By this time they were more experienced at braking the wagons with brush and extra oxen at the back of the wagon. Loading and unloading wagons could be done much faster.

Reaching tiny Fort Bridger, situated on Green River in Wyoming, they rested and repaired the ravages of the trip. The dilapidated fort consisted of two houses held together with poles and daubed with mud. The emigrants described the adobe houses as a shabby concern with sod roofs. About twenty-five trappers' lodges were occupied with Indian wives and children. Jim Bridger, a famous mountainman, when faced with the decline of the beaver, had built this small fort in the path of the emigrant road. It soon became the second best supply depot for the thousands of pioneers. However, the fort's meager store of provisions was soon depleted when the long lines of wagon trains began. To supplement the supply of food, the scouts understanding the Indians better than the pioneers, bartered with the nearby Indians for food.

Many disgruntled travelers, weary to the bone and disenchanted by dire warnings of restless Indians, hunger and thirst ahead, elected to take the California Trail, touted to be easier and closer. Some religious groups were traveling to the big lake in Utah Territory. After two days of rest, a smaller train set out for Oregon. It was heartbreaking to leave friends behind. The Elliotts and the Brandons had both decided to stay the course.

Late in August the wagon train, smaller now that so many wagons had branched off on the California Trail, rolled joyfully into Soda Springs. Located near Idaho's Bear River, the lush, green meadow was already dotted with many tents and wagons. As Zeke and Jed searched for the best camping site, the rest of the party gaped at the bounty that was so pleasing to the eyes. After so many months of dust, mud, and scorching heat, big smiles of delight brightened their faces. Luxuriant streams, bordered by leafy willow trees offering shade, ringed the lush mountain meadow. The scene appeared to be a mirage just waiting for the weary party. Refreshing springs seemed to bubble from the earth. Eager men began to unyoke the oxen, unsaddle the horses and turn them out to munch the lush, green grass. Zeke rode his tired horse around the encampment to let them know they would be resting here for three days. He told them the next step along the trail after Fort Hall, would be along the rugged Snake River Canyons, and the travel would be difficult.

"Folks, we'll be needing all our strength to tackle that part of the trail!"

Wood was gathered, fires built, and delicious smells wafted on the air. Basic supplies were running low, but everyone wanted to make this evening a celebration. Now that the women had more time to cook, they unpacked little used ovens, and baked biscuits and cornbread. Ingenious cooks mixed the water from the springs, containing soda, in their biscuits to make them rise. Some rare dried apple pies, and even some cakes appeared that night. Men removed the tailgates on some of the wagons, and laid them over barrels to make tables, in anticipation of a delicious supper.

Other men and some of the older boys went fishing and brought back fresh, thick mountain trout. Those who had forgotten to bring fish hooks with them on the trip, borrowed some from an emigrant who had brought along a gross of hooks. The younger boys, not occupied with chores, were set to work catching lively grasshoppers for bait. After the fish were cleaned the women fried them in huge frying pans called spiders. This is a large pan used for frying which stands over the fire on metal legs, and reminds one of a black spider.

The younger women and girls had gone berry picking on this pleasant August day. Others took baskets and dug wild onions to give a new flavor to the stews. Laughter and happy conversation was a delightful pastime, while everyone rested and relaxed. Spirited music and dancing were enjoyed that night.

Some men too shy to ask women to dance, donned aprons or bandannas tied under their chins to mark them as the female partner, and danced with other men accompanied by much laughter. Watchers laughed so hard it brought tears to their eyes. Livelier music caused spirited jigs to break out with Jed, a borrowed apron around his waist, dancing the part of the lady. There were few women on the frontier, and less entertainment. Lonely men, loving to dance and play music, adapted to the scarcity of women by recruiting someone to play the part of the lady in the dance. After dancing a lively reel, Jed wiped his brow and declared that supper must be ready.

Jed exclaimed, "the food was fit for the Gods," after his third helping. Unable to eat more food, the men sat back on their heels, gazed at the harvest moon, and listened to the croaking of the frogs in contentment.

The hard worked oxen, cattle, and horses browsed gratefully in the thick grass. Quincy joined the other dogs romping around the camp, voicing their own pleasure. Samson, eagerly lapping a saucer of milk Cordelia had traded from another train for some dried meat, kept a wary eye on the whereabouts of the excited dogs. Three of the surviving pigs, much larger now, dug their snoots in the grass searching for tasty roots. Darlin' amused himself by chewing a strip of rawhide used to tie a water barrel on someone's wagon. Enjoying the unaccustomed rest, the good food and the entertainment, most merrymakers stayed up late but finally drifted off to bed.

Captain Quarles kept the members busy the next day. Many repairs were made to the wagons and harnesses. Sore feet and hooves were given needed attention. Knowing the way ahead would be hard on the oxen's hooves, the tar mixture was painted on and left to dry to strengthen them. Bent metal rims that circled the wheels were hammered out. Some iron wheels and wooden spokes needed to be replaced. Dirty clothes were scrubbed on washboards, rinsed, dried and repaired. Children ran to and fro, screaming their delight. Feeling free to explore, they scouted the area's more interesting spots. Baskets of berries were picked and put out on cloths to dry. Wild strawberries, blackberries, salmonberries, gooseberries, huckleberries, currants, and plums were stuffed into mouths, until hands, faces, and clothes were stained with red and purple juices. Sarah Ann and Jonathan, laughingly fed each other berries and clearly enjoyed each other's company.

Thinking more of providing food for the caravan, the men gathered to talk while they cleaned and oiled their guns in preparation to go hunting. Some who would have liked to go along were asked to stay and keep a cautious eye on the camp. They had no luck hunting bear, but managed to bag a couple of elk and several ducks as well as a few geese. Someone joked that it was a good thing they hadn't seen any bear. There were many stories on the frontier about the horrors experienced by some who had attempted to shoot a bear.

Using one of the tables they had set up, the men began to clean and skin the game. In order to be fair in sharing the fresh meat, it was cut, then placed on the tables in small piles. Some choice pieces, and some not so choice pieces, were placed in each pile. When all was ready, the men who had families, were called together and asked to turn their backs so they could not see the table of meat.

Captain Quarles would then point to a pile of meat, saying, "Who'll take this pile?"

One of the assembled men, not being able to see, but hoping that it was a good pile, would call out, "I will." In this manner all the meat piles were given out fairly. Some piles were not as good as others, but no one seemed to know a fairer method. Several women dried some meat strips over the smoky campfire. During the trip, hunters always made sure the neediest families were given the small game.

9

Horace scooped up one of the geese, carried it over to Mrs. Kincaid's wagon, and tossed it on the ground. Scratching under his itchy buckskin shirt and thinking about eating juicy, hot goose meat for his next meal, he drawled, "That there's for you, woman. You can pull those feathers off and cook it for my supper."

Mrs. Kincaid gave Horace a long level look, dipped into her snuff box, placed a dip in her mouth, and replied saucily, "If you want to eat it, you clean it."

"I declare! Did anyone ever tell you that you can catch more flies with honey than you can with vinegar?" Horace asked, with a twinkle in his eye. He loved to get a response from his teasing.

"Yep. My mother told me. That's why I always use vinegar. What sane woman would want to draw flies!"

Horace guffawed, and slapped his hands in glee. Samson jumped down off the wagon seat to check out the limp goose, sniffed, then looked up at Mrs. Kincaid expectantly.

"I guess you won that battle, Horace. Samson loves goose turned on a spit so I'll clean that straggly feathered critter this time. But, just you look out for next time. By the way, you can turn the spit." Cordelia walked away chuckling to herself, as Horace grinned and rolled his smoke.

All the necessary chores were done, so on the third day most everyone felt like playing. The younger children scattered to scout the area near the creek. Both the boys and girls had the same idea. How delicious it would feel to go swimming. The boys found a section down the creek aways that was very deep. Looking longingly at the cool water they all began to tear off their clothes.

"Wait a minute," despaired Ben, "I don't have on any underwear. Mine was all wore out, so I used them to grease the wheels." Several other boys agreed they weren't wearing underwear, either.

"Back home we used to run down to the naked hole to wash off after we got done plowing."

"I know what! We'll call it the naked hole, then we can all go swimming!"

"No one's looking anyhow," declared Ben.

"Let's do it!" "Last one in is a horned toad!"

Splash!

Into the deep pool went the dare-devil boys. They swam joyfully with big grins on their wet, dripping faces, playfully pushing each other under the water. Even daring to dive off the high limbs of an overhanging willow tree. Ben was the most daring of all, diving off the highest limb. None of the other boys were brave enough to attempt such a feat. Pushing wet hair out of their eyes, they laughed at each others silly antics.

Up the creek aways, Rachel and the younger girls had found a place deep enough for swimming. Because they had been taught to always act like ladies, they kept on their chemises and bloomers. Since they had forgotten to bring any soap they washed their hair with sand. (In truth, they knew that if they had asked for soap and permission to go swimming, their mothers would have said, "No!") Splashing and giggling in the refreshing water, the girls forgot the time.

"I hear a dog barking nearby," one of the girls exclaimed!

"Maybe someone's coming," another girl screeched!

Screaming in mock fright they ran, dripping, out of the water, grabbed their clothes from the bushes, and put them on over their wet underclothes.

"It sounds like Quincy. He ran off and left us earlier."

"Let's go find out why he's barking."

They ran barefoot down the creek toward the sound of barking. Rachel wondered what was bothering her little pet. As they neared the spot where they could see Quincy barking, Rachel put her finger on her lips and whispered, "Sh-sh-sh, be very quiet." They all pulled back branches, and peeked through at the unwary boys splashing in the deep pool. The girls' eyes bugged out, mouths dropped open, as they began to laugh out loud at the sight.

Shock, then dismay registered on the boy's faces, as they ran frantically for cover. Jumping quickly into their clothes, the boys emerged from the bushes looking quite embarrassed at their discovery.

"You won't tell will you?" a worried boy asked.

"We'll get switched for sure if you do," warned one of Ben's friends.

"You should have *SEEN* Ben dive off that highest limb way up yonder," one of his friends boasted as he pointed at the limb. As the other boys turned to gawk at him, his face turned a bright red, as he remembered Ben hadn't been wearing any clothes at the time.

"I me..a..n," he began to stutter.

"We *KNOW* what you meant."

"You must be joking! Dive off that limb way up there. No way!" The laughing girls agreed with Rachel. It just couldn't be done.

"If I had swimming trunks, I'd show you I can do it," Ben boasted.

"Well, Mr. Smarty, I'll lend you my bloomers, then we'll see." Rachel gasped at her nerve to say such a thing to Ben. But, with the other girls looking on with smirks on their faces, she just couldn't back down.

"We'll dare you to do it!" the girls chorused.

"Double dog dare you," cried the excited boys.

"You bet!" agreed Benjamin. "I'll take you all on," he replied, as he wondered how he had gotten himself into this fix.

Sarah and her friends went behind some bushes to pull off her wet bloomers while the girls giggled. Too shy to come out, they tossed them out to the waiting boys. With his friends circled around him as a shield, Benjamin donned the flimsy bloomers. Trying to help, the boy's nervous fingers made them too clumsy to be much help with the wet clothing. Knowing he was in for it now, Ben put on a bold front and came strutting out of the circle to confront the girls.

"Ready to back down?" one girl called out.

"He's stalling," claimed another.

"We're waiting," the girls chorused.

Feeling trapped, but determined not to embarrass himself any further, he began to climb the tree. The loose bloomers snagged several times on a limb as he worked his way slowly to the top of the tree. Perched on the limb with both his arms raised to dive, he looked down on the laughing upturned faces. With a dejected sigh, he gave a mighty shove against the limb, and dove head first toward the pool below. Air shooshed into the bloomers as he descended, causing them to blow up like a balloon. Twisting around in midair to keep from losing the bloomers, he landed, "SPLAT" in the water. A wave splashed up on the muddy shore at the children's feet.

Everyone watched for his head to bob up. Nothing! Just when his friends were getting ready to dive in after him, the top of his head peeked out of the water.

"Are you hurt?" someone asked.

"Come on out," another called.

"I can't!" Benjamin choked out.

"Why not?" they chorused.

"Cause I've lost the bloomers, that's why."

Snickers, giggles, and hearty laughter broke out on the bank.

"Sh..sh..sh, someone's coming."

Quincy had started to bark again as his sharp eyes looked back toward the encampment. Striding toward the creek was Benjamin's father carrying some buckets. Calamity! They were in for it now. Dripping wet, and too scared to move, Ben could only stand nose deep in the water and stare at his father.

"What's going on here?" his father asked gruffly.

"We were just swimming, sir." answered one of the braver boys.

"Why is Benjamin still standing in the water?" his father asked, puzzled at the children's actions.

"He can't come out, sir. He's lost his bloomers!"

The girls smothered a giggle. The boys snickered. His father glared. Sizing up the situation while watching the embarrassed laughter and red faces, Samuel quickly dispatched one of the boys to the camp for a pair of trousers for Benjamin. Next, he sent the disgraced girls on their way.

"My son, I've got a feeling you won't be sitting down for a week!" he called out to Benjamin, who was still standing silently in the water. Grinning, he remembered some of his own escapades when he was ten years old.

Sure enough, the boys all got a switching that evening, back at the camp. The emigrants grinned at all the hollering they heard, saying. "It will do them good. Boys mustn't be allowed to run wild." The girls were more fortunate as no one squealed on their unladylike behavior.

After resting at Soda Springs for three days, the well rested, impatient company was ready to depart on the next phase of their journey. They had been told that Fort Hall was only twenty to thirty miles away. No one seemed to know the exact distance. Earlier than usual that morning, the oxen had been yoked in place, and all the packing was finished in record time. After breakfast, the men decided to have a last minute meeting.

Some of the children ran down to the creek to play for a few more minutes. Rachel and Quincy were walking with the other girls her age, when they heard the call, "Let's roll!"

One of the girls called back as she began to run, "I bet I can beat you all to the train!"

All of the girls took off racing for the camp. As Rachel ran as fast as her legs would carry her, she caught sight of Quincy out of the corner of her eye. He was chasing a prairie dog through the woods away from the train. She slid to a halt, looked after the disappearing girls, noted where Quincy had vanished, and quickly decided to take a few minutes to fetch Quincy. Sure the wagon train wouldn't leave without her, she ran while her eyes searched this way and that, but she couldn't find Quincy.

Finally she saw his tracks in the mud near a boggy area. "I'm getting close now," she thought. Feeling tired, she sat down on a boulder for a few minutes before trudging on. Every few minutes she would call weakly, "Here, Quincy!" Convinced she would find him soon, she continued to look, sensing her time was running out. Surely they wouldn't leave without her.

Rachel collapsed hopelessly on the cold ground. Tears were streaming down her face. She knew she would have to give up the search. Quincy was lost to her. She would have to leave him out here alone in this desolate wilderness. "Poor Quincy," she thought dismally as her tired eyes closed in sleep.

10

Rachel woke with a start. "How long have I slept," she wondered. As she glanced around to get her bearings, she saw a horse and rider coming toward her. Thinking it was one of the men from the wagon train come to fetch her, she began to walk toward him. Rachel stopped in her tracks, and gasped in alarm.

Approaching her was an Indian! His long black hair was slicked back in front, braided with feathers, and hung down his back. He wore only a loin cloth and knee-high moccasins and a western style vest. An assortment of beads and teeth hung around his neck. His horse had some circular painted patterns, a blanket for a saddle, and a pack hanging down one side. Sliding down from his horse, he looked at her with a fierce-looking scowl on his face. Speaking some strange sounding words that she couldn't understand, he gestured with his hand. In the other hand, he held a long feathered lance that he waved in the air, frightening her. She felt he meant to kill her. Whirling away, she began to run, but he was faster. He knocked her to the ground, then caught her hands bringing them behind her back, and tied them tightly with a rawhide string.

In one swift motion, he swung her up on his horse and mounted behind her. Clucking to the horse, the Indian rode through the trees, then went past the deep pool in the creek where she and her friends had embarrassed the boys. The sturdy horse carried them easily up the bank to where the wagon train had camped. Nothing but the blackened camp fires were left to show anyone had been there. How could they go off and abandon her? Desolate, she dropped her head and let her salty tears fall, dampening the front of her dress. The Indian looked at her, shook his head, and pointed the way the wagons had gone. Again, he spoke in a sound she couldn't understand. After giving a long searching look down the wagon wheel rutted trail, he turned his horse and headed back into the trees.

What would happen to a White hostage in an Indian village? How soon would he kill her? Terrible thoughts swirled through her mind. She remembered grisly stories she had heard about captives being forced to do hard labor with little food. Would she be a slave and be beaten frequently? Was this what her future held? She was only a little girl, surely he wouldn't hurt her, would he?

It seemed like hours later, her head bobbing as she half slept, when she heard a noise off in the distance. At first she couldn't tell what kind of noise it was. It sounded like barking. Quincy! Was somebody coming to save her? Suddenly, out of the bushes rushed an excited Quincy, snarling and yelping at the horse and rider. The wild horse pranced in agitation and tried to wound Quincy with his hooves. Raising the feathered lance high in the air, her captor looked for an opportunity to strike the charging dog. Screaming as loud as she could, she managed to poke her elbows into his chest, making him grunt. While waving her arms in the air and shaking her head, she managed to distract the startled Indian.

"Quincy! Down boy!" she called out desperately. Quincy, trained to obey her commands, sat down on his haunches, whined, and looked up at Rachel wistfully. Turning her head to appeal to the Indian for mercy, her eyes looked deeply into his.

Was that kindness she saw? Of course not, he was an Indian, not capable of kindness, she judged. Speaking to her in that strange language, he placed his hand on her shoulder, as he lowered the lance. Leaning down a strong arm, he scooped up the small dog and handed him to Rachel, who hugged him tightly. At least, now she wasn't all alone. She knew Quincy would do his best to protect her.

All that day they traveled until the horse was weary. The hot August sun beat down on Rachel's tired body. Her eyes scanned the trees and bushes for some sign of where they were. She knew she had not seen this wild region before. If only she knew what direction they were traveling. Her grumbling stomach wouldn't let her forget how much she suffered with pangs of hunger.

Frequently the Indian had set Quincy on the ground to run along beside the trotting horse until his little legs tired. Then he would scoop him up again and place him back in her arms. Rachel had nodded off several times during the day and came awake with a sudden jerk of her head. Her small body suffered many discomforts because of the tight bindings and the restrictions of being held captive on the jolting horse.

The sky was beginning to darken into a beautiful sunset before the tireless Indian halted his horse to make camp for the night. Rachel was even more afraid now. What did he mean to do with her? His bare arms reached up and dragged the exhausted, struggling girl from the horse's back. Quincy fell to the ground and ran around, barking frantically. The Indian calmed his agitated horse as he tied it to a nearby limb, then turned his fierce gaze on Rachel. He gestured for her to silence the dog. Somehow understanding what he meant, she calmed Quincy. Untying her hands, he rubbed some feeling back into them. Indicating she should go behind a large bush, he turned his back while she straightened her clothes and tried to get herself together. Finished, she walked out into the small clearing. He had taken the pack off the horse and placed the horse blanket on the ground in front of a small tree. Pointing and grunting for her to sit down, he took his rawhide rope and tied her to the tree.

Picking up his bow and arrow, he disappeared from sight. Surely he wouldn't leave her tied up and alone out here in the wilderness to starve to death! Or even worse, left to be eaten by wild animals! Her head sagged on her chest as the salty tears began to flow down her cheeks. Saddened at his master's actions, Quincy crawled up on Rachel's stomach and fell asleep. Tired from the difficult day, Rachel also drowsed.

The Indian moved stealthily as he approached the tiny clearing. His eyes scanned the area for anything out of the ordinary. Convinced nothing had changed since he had left, he began to search the glen for wood to build a campfire. Soon a fire burned brightly, with almost no smoke to send a warning of someone's presence. Crouched before the fire, he took his knife from its sheathe, and began to clean the rabbit he had killed for their supper. He placed sticks in front of the fire and carefully pierced the rabbit so it would cook over the coals. Soon, a delicious smell wafted out to Rachel's nose, as she awakened with a start. Walking to her side, he untied her from the tree and wound the rope around her wrists again, while Quincy growled. She got to her feet and walked around the small camp to stretch her legs, with Quincy following her every step. The Indian watched and frowned until he understood she wasn't trying to get away. She laughed under her breath, "Where could she go? She didn't even know which way to head."

Finally, he motioned her to sit down by the fire. Alarmed, she quickly did what he wanted. Taking the hot food from the fire, he ripped off a leg and pushed it at her, again talking in a guttural sound she couldn't understand. The saliva began to run, as the delicious smell of the meat reached her nose. She shook her head, no, but he pushed it at her again. "I think he means for me to eat," she thought longingly. Quincy's alert eyes watched the dripping meat as his tongue lolled out the side of his mouth. Rachel had never been hungrier in her life. As her stomach growled, she reached out with her bound hands and accepted the juicy morsel. Her teeth ripped at the meat, as she greedily devoured the meal. A skin of water was handed to her, and she drank deeply of the warm water. The Indian finished his meal, tossed the scraps to a grateful Quincy, then wiped his hands on his vest. Rachel looked at her greasy hands, mimicked her captor, and wiped her hands on her clothes.

Her head sagged, then her eyes closed in sleep. The Indian reached over and lightly punched her arm. Her body jerked awake in alarm. As her eyes looked wildly at her captor in fear, he motioned for her to sleep on the blanket. He rose and stalked off into the trees. Exhausted, she lay down and pulled the dirty blanket around her as best she could. Quincy's bright eyes gazed in the direction the Indian had taken, then curled up close to her to guard her from the darkness.

She woke several times during the night, her bound hands cutting off the circulation, aching too much to sleep. Looking up at the bright stars and harvest moon, she wondered if she would ever see her family again. She didn't think her mother could stand losing two of her children. Why did such a peaceful looking world have so many problems that caused so many people pain. Listening to the yip of coyotes, she sighed, wiggled on the hard ground, found a softer spot, and dropped off to sleep.

Quincy's warning growl woke her just before dawn as the Indian walked back into the clearing. Pointing to her and then to a nearby bush, he made her understand his meaning. Trying to get to her feet was difficult, her body was so stiff and sore. She felt bruised but he hadn't abused her. Yet! She stumbled behind the bush and nearly fell. When she came back, the Indian had thrown the blanket on the horse and was ready to ride. By this time her spirit was so low, she didn't care where he was taking her. At least he was letting her keep Quincy. He had been kind to the little dog, handing him up for her to hold when his short legs got tired. Swinging her up on the Indian pony with his strong arm, he mounted swiftly behind her, kicked the horse into motion with his heels, and galloped out of the clearing. Quincy followed as fast as he could run.

Rachel's strength was fading. The hot sun seemed to melt her bones. The constant jolting of the horse, hunger, thirst, not to mention fear, were quickly taking their toll. Only the Indian's powerful arms kept her from falling off the plodding horse, as she clutched a weary Quincy close to her body. Her fragile sense of pride was damaged, and her constant loneliness left her close to tears. Now her little devoted pet was her only family, and she must hold on to him for dear life. Without him, she could easily lose the fine thread of sanity.

As she drowsed, the horse came to a stop, then the Indian slid off dragging her down with him. He stood her up on her numb feet and motioned for her to walk around. A cool stream was nearby in a delightful shady grove. He strode to the stream, filled his skin canteen with cool water, and brought it back for her to drink her fill. Then he spread the horse blanket on the ground so she could rest. After Rachel made herself as comfortable as she could, she gazed at the Indian with half-closed eyes. First he led the horse to the stream to drink, then staked him out to graze. Taking some dried meat from a pack, he turned and offered some to her. Noticing a necklace of bear claws around his neck, she decided to call him, Bearclaw. After all, he hadn't hurt her, and he was kind to Quincy. As she lay on the dirty horse blanket she stared at the inky blackness of the night and listened to the night sounds. Hungry, her hair filthy, her clothes dirty and tattered, Rachel scratched at her itchy skin as she despaired of ever seeing her family again. Clutching Quincy tightly, her eyes gradually closed in fretful sleep. At dawn, they set out again. He seemed to have a destination in mind, but they could not communicate with each other. Several times their eyes locked as if he wished he could tell her something, but could not.

* * * *

It was well into the day's travel before Rachel was missed. Jed rode Darlin' up to the Brandon's wagon and called out, "It's just old Jed and Darlin' come to take you for a ride, Rachel honey."

Darlin' stretched her neck down to the wagon as her teeth began to gnaw at the boards. "Stop that, you rascal! You'll get splinters in yore stomach," Jed complained, as he pulled her head away from the wagon with the reins.

Rebeccah still feeling poorly, poked her head out and said, "She's not here, Jed. She must be walking behind with Sarah Ann and her friends."

"Naw, she ain't there. Darlin' checked there first." Sudden alarm showed on his face. "I'll just go check with the Captain." Dust from the trail flew as he kicked Darlin' into a run. His eyes scanned the wagons as he located the Captain talking with Zeke, as they rode along near the head of the column. Waving his hat to get their attention, he rode up and slid Darlin' to a halt.

"Anyone of y'all seen Rachel today?"

"No, I haven't," the Captain drawled, while wiping sweat out of his eyes with his bandanna. "I just got back from scouting up ahead. How about you, Zeke?"

"Not since early this morning, back at the camp. Why are you lookin' for her, Jed?"

"Tarnation!" exclaimed Jed in exasperation, as he scratched his neck under his red long johns. "She's missing, that's why!"

"Missing?

"I said that, didn't I? You deaf or something?"

"Now, don't get yourself all riled up, Jed. If she's truly missing, we'll mount a search and find her real soon. She's probably waitin' back down the trail aways." The trio rode off toward the wagons to round up some men to search for the lost child. Not wanting to take too many men and leave the train unprotected, a search party of four packed some supplies, and with Jed and Darlin' leading the search, rode past all the wagons. As they galloped back down trail, the wagon train continued westward toward Fort Hall.

All day the searchers looked for Rachel. After an exhausting ride, they came upon their deserted, forlorn looking, morning camp. No Rachel waiting for rescue. Jed gathered some wood and built a fire on top of an old campfire. Horace hobbled the horses and set them to grazing nearby. They made coffee, and cooked some bacon and pan bread, hoping the smell would bring a frightened Rachel out of the woods. Tossing the dregs of his coffee on the fire, Jed advised, "We'll camp here tonight and strike her trail in the morning. Best lay down your pallet and get some rest, Jonathan."

The youthful pioneer had demanded he be allowed to join the search, when he heard Rachel was missing. When Hank Brandon had insisted on going with Jed, and Horace had volunteered, Jonathan had called, "I'll go, if I can borrow my Pa's horse." To his credit he had kept up the fast pace all day with the older, more experienced men without complaint. As they made plans for the next day, Jonathan dropped off to sleep thinking that Sarah Ann would be proud of him.

"Lookee yonder, the boy's asleep. Samuel should be mighty proud of that young'un." Soon Hank went to his pallet to try to get some sleep, if he could. Discussing the situation in whispers, Horace and Jed having more frontier experience, feared the worst had happened to Rachel. They curled up for warmth in their bedrolls but slept lightly. Horace jokingly called it, "Sleeping with one eye open!"

Dawn found Jed at the creek washing his face and getting water for coffee. The fire had burned down to hot coals. Gently nudging Jonathan with the toe of his moccasin, he called, "Time to rise and shine, young'un! We best be on our way."

After a meager breakfast, the men mounted and rode to investigate the creek and the surrounding area. It was nearly noon when Jed dismounted and called Horace to come look at what he had found. A tiny scrap of faded blue calico hung from a tree branch. Scanning the area with sharp eyes, Jed called the men's attention to tiny tracks on the ground.

"Looks like Quincy's tracks, alright. Appears he was running." Hank offered his opinion that Rachel was lost, but she still had Quincy with her.

"Nope, ain't so," claimed Jed. "How tall is Rachel? This hyar scrap was as high up as me on my horse. My guess is someone's got her and he's on horseback. Kaint find no mark of a horseshoe so it's probably an Indian," Jed remarked as his eyes scanned the ground. "Reckon we best head on back to the train. We can ask for help at Fort Hall. This hyar little party kaint take on no Indians! Let's ride!"

11

After three months of exhausting travel, the wagon train rolled into Fort Hall, in Idaho Territory. The 80 foot square trading post built in 1834, by Nathanial J. Wyeth, Boston trader and world traveler, was constructed from cottonwood logs, then later enlarged with sun-dried bricks. Here the travelers were discouraged from continuing their trek northwest along the Snake and Columbia Rivers, then on to the Willamette Valley. Captain Richard Grant, who worked for the English based Hudson's Bay Fur Trading Company, tried to discourage Americans from continuing to Oregon. He felt that more Americans in the Oregon Territory would conflict with the hopes of the Territory becoming British. By telling the emigrants how hazardous the trail was, many settlers opted to continue on across Nevada to California. Dr. Marcus Whitman's talks back East, had persuaded the emigrants that in order to hold the West for America, the Oregon wilderness must be settled. Taking his advice under consideration, most of the emigrants opted to take the wagon train on to Oregon, the land of their dreams.

Captain Quarles reported Rachel missing. Asked if anyone had been sent out to look for her, the Captain answered, "Yes, four good men went out searching two days ago for her, but we haven't seen them since. Two are experienced scouts. Have you heard of any Indian trouble in these hyar parts lately?"

"Well, the tribes ain't in a uproar, but there's always trouble somewhere," answered the man behind the counter. His job was a combination of peace keeper, Indian Agent, fur trader, and shopkeeper. He tried his best to keep the busy fort stocked with supplies. But, with hundreds of wagons passing by expecting to be resupplied, his job was nearly impossible.

"If they don't bring her in, we'll send out a party of searchers to look for the little gal. That's about all we can do to help. Can't guarantee finding her, though," the agent sympathized.

"Thankee, sir. Can't ask any more than that," the Captain answered as he looked around for a spittoon. Outside the fort, emigrants camped and tried to get on with their daily business until the wagon train moved again. Women visited with neighbors, trying to keep up with what was going on back East. Back home where it was civilized, many thought.

In the Brandon wagon, Rebeccah was so distraught she couldn't cook or even cope with her life. She felt she had been abandoned in the wilderness. She could not, no, would not live through this terrible turmoil. Losing Baby Andrew was bad enough but to lose another child, not knowing whether she was alive or dead, or...captured! At the thought, Rebeccah shuddered and fresh tears began to fall.

Sarah Ann, her own heart breaking, stayed at her mother's side as much as she could, trying to reassure her that everything would be alright. Jed, Horace, her father, and Jonathan would find her sister if anyone could. She knew she didn't have a right to be, but she was worried about Jonathan being out there as well as her lost sister. He was young and inexperienced in the vast wilderness and could get himself lost or captured. Jonathan was such a nice young man. Jed had whispered to Sarah Ann when Jonathan had volunteered to go on the search party, "Don't worry none, little missy. I'll keep my one good eye on him. Darlin' will look after him, too. She thinks you two are the cutest couple."

Sarah Ann's face had blushed a brilliant scarlet, but she grinned and bravely waved goodby to the search party.

Cordelia Kincaid had been very kind to the Brandon family. She brought food, hope, a bright personality, encouragement, and a tiny handmade, lace edged headache pillow to put under Rebeccah's aching head. In Hank's absence, his beloved Becky, needed compassion from friends and loved ones. Other women on the train tried their best to cheer Rebeccah. All she could do in her despair was to look out from her covered wagon home and observe the Indians around the fort. Most of them wore a bright combination of Indian and western clothes. Indian tepees and crude trapper huts were everywhere she looked. Indian women and their children, scouts in their buckskins, traders of every kind, dogs, oxen, cattle and horses, were all living in close proximity with the emigrants. Everything looked so dismal, that it was very hard to hold on to any hope that Rachel would be found.

"Riders, yo!" Someone called. Eyes swiveled to the horizon in the direction the wagon train had come. They were too far off yet to see if Rachel was with them. As the four riders approached, it was obvious that they were alone. Sad eyes watched the dusty men swing down from their tired, sweaty horses.

"Another sweet soul lost to her family," the onlookers thought to themselves. Hank hurried to his wagon to comfort his Becky. His tormented eyes seemed to look through those friends who greeted him. He disappeared into the wagon as his friends drifted out of sight and hearing to give the bereaved couple privacy.

*   *   *   *

Rachel looked at the pale moon bathing the forest glen in dim light. As she watched, coyotes yapped in the distance making her shiver in fear. An owl perched on a nearby limb, called loudly. "Wh-oo! Wh-oo!" She was getting used to the owl's hooting call. It barely made her jump anymore. Glancing over at Bearclaw,

111

she scratched under her dirty, torn dress and wished she could have a bath. They had stopped midday to rest the horse, and he had taken off the rope around her wrists. Turning her wrists over in his big callused hands, he grimaced at the raw, bloody sores. She looked up into his dark brown eyes and thought she saw...what? Was that concern?...Worry? The awful stories she had heard came rushing back into her head, as she jerked her hands away. He handed her a piece of dried meat, then lifted her up on the horse's back as he scowled at her fiercely. Leaping up behind her he grunted for Quincy to follow.

By evening, she was exhausted and nearly fell off the tired horse. Quincy had made it through another day of riding, then nearly running his little legs off. Bearclaw gathered wood for a fire and cooked some kind of stew for their dinner. It was unlike anything she had ever eaten before. He brought her dinner on a wooden plate he had whittled while waiting for the food to cook. Making guttural sounds and hand signals, he indicated she should eat. Funny, but she was beginning to understand what he wanted her to do. This night he allowed her to place the horse's blanket on the ground where she wanted to sleep. As she snuggled down with Quincy curled up against her, she knew she should be sleeping, but there was just too much on her mind tonight. Her body was weary from bouncing on a horse all day. Even though Bearclaw frightened her, he hadn't hurt her. Except for her battered wrists, and tired body she was alright. He hadn't killed her...yet! But, where was he taking her? Gently her eyes closed and she fell asleep.

*   *   *   *

Jed and Horace had made a pact with Hank not to tell his Becky about the Indian sign they had seen back at the Soda Springs camp. Walking around the fort with Sarah Ann on his arm, Jonathan had taken her into his confidence and told her there was probably no hope for Rachel. He dried her tears with an old torn handkerchief, as he told her he'd heard they were moving on the next day. It seemed to her that no one really *CARED* what had happened to Rachel. She was dead to them now.

Daylight brought activity in the camp. Smoke rose in the brisk morning atmosphere. Soon the good smells of breakfast cooking filled the cool air. Jed led Darlin' up to the campfire. Darlin' pushed her nose around and nudged Jed's shoulder as he tried to throw the saddle over her back. "Stop that, or I'll give you away to the next wild mountainman I see!" Jed chuckled as he pushed her head out of his way with his black gloved hand. "You acting mighty frisky this morning. I'm feeling a mite tuckered myself. These hyar old bones can feel winter comin' on fast. If I recollect correctly, and by the look of those leaves on yonder tree, we're into September already." Jed shivered, reached to take the makings out of his shirt pocket, and began to roll a cigarette. One of the pigs looking for breakfast began to nibble at Darlin's hoof. She snorted, kicked her heels and snapped at the pesky pig. The squealing pig made a fast get-a-way while the onlookers laughed. Jed remarked, "That was the first time I laughed since Rachel...uh...disappeared!"

Rebeccah had begged to be left behind to wait for Rachel. Everyone discouraged her. Hank said she must continue on to Oregon even though her heart was breaking. Members were saying their last goodbyes to friends they had made on the trail, and to new friends they had made at Fort Hall. The wagons were lined up facing west and all drivers were ready, when the call came down the line, "Let's roll!" Looking back down the trail, Rebeccah choking with tears, whispered, "Goodbye, Rachel! We loved you so."

All they had heard about the terrible Snake River Canyons made them tremble in fear. Knowing they were nearing the end of their journey, and could claim land and start a new beginning in the West, gave them courage they didn't know they possessed. The women wrapped shawls around themselves and shivered in the crisp early September morning. The emigrants were all abuzz with the news that soon another California group would be heading southwest, at the fork of the trails, near Raft River. It was expected that they would "noon" there. Bonnetted women gossiped about home as they walked along behind the train. What would happen to their lives, if ever they reached their new home, was rarely discussed.

*   *   *   *

Rachel helped Bearclaw gather wood for their breakfast fire, and place the blanket on the horse's back. He still watched every move she made, but only got upset when she wandered too close to the edge of the clearing. Then he would jabber, and motion with his arms, for her to stay in the center of the glen. This morning, he reached into a skin bag and with a hooked whittled wooden spoon, dipped out a funny-looking substance, and indicated she should open her mouth. Knowing how angry he got when she didn't follow his commands, she opened and took the smelly stuff into her mouth. It contained some kind of dried meat, berries, and some sort of fat, and was ground into a powder. It didn't taste too bad. He handed her the make-shift spoon and let her eat as much as she wanted, which wasn't very much. After they ate, they carefully put out the fire, picked up the camp, then mounted the horse and rode at a gallop toward her destiny.

*   *   *   *

The wagon train circled for their noon stop. Only when they didn't feel safe from Indian attack would they circle the wagons for safety at noon. The heavy wagons provided some protection from arrows and bullets. Sometimes they would keep on the move and eat a cold lunch. But it was more convenient for the women to cook, since many shared cooking chores with each other. As the men unyoked the oxen so they could graze, the women gathered wood and built cooking fires. Hunters had brought in some game while they rested at Fort Hall, so many families enjoyed fried venison with gravy over biscuits for their noon meal. After they ate, the women cleaned up while the men rolled smokes or chewed tobacco and rested in the warm sun. They were ready to say their final goodbyes to the California Train, when Zeke's sharp eyes picked up something different on the horizon. Whatever it was looked hazy in the sunlight. Kind of wavy and distorted. As soon as he could tell what the image was, he called out in alarm, "Rider coming in fast! Looks like an Indian. Better alert the camp!"

Wary men made sure their guns were ready to fire, as women and children ran for cover behind the wagons. Dogs, cattle, pigs and chickens scattered everywhere. The chickens were let out of their wire cages as often as possible, then coaxed back in with a few grains of precious corn. Horace hurriedly tied a nervous Samson to Cordelia's wagon seat to keep him out of the way. The Indian was riding closer to the camp. All eyes were on him now. He had slowed his horse to a walk, being very cautious not to alarm the emigrants. It looked like a sleeping child slumped in front of him.

A loud scream came from inside the corral. Men grabbed for their guns. Someone yelled, "It's a trick! We're being attacked!" Becky ran holding up her skirts, screeching like she had lost her mind, straight toward the Indian. His horse reared up on its hind legs, frantic to escape. Holding the child in his arms, he slid off the rear of the horse in a fluid motion, keeping hold of the reins. The stunned emigrants watched as Becky grabbed the child from the Indian, then ran straight into Hank's waiting arms. Thinking that Becky was stealing the Indian child to replace her own lost child, the men pulled their guns on the Indian, who stood very still. All eyes stared at the filthy child. With eyes as big as saucers, she stared back. Quincy, seeing familiar faces, wiggled out of her limp arms, dropped to the ground and went romping around in circles, barking delightedly.

Jed cried out, "My God, it's Rachel!"

Everyone, but the men holding guns on the Indian, crowded around the little girl clutched in her mother's arms. It was hard to recognize her through all the dirt and torn clothing, but it was Rachel alright, with a big smile plastered on her face. Everyone had to give her kisses and big hugs. She glanced up to see what had happened to Bearclaw, and saw the watchful men glaring, and holding him at gunpoint. Rachel left her mother's arms, strolled through the crowd of her friends to where the frightened Indian stood his ground, reached up and took his large hand in hers. The crowd gasped in awe! She led him over to her father and began to tell her story.

"At first I thought he was kidnapping me, and I was real scared. But he didn't hurt me, except where the ropes cut into the skin of my wrists, and made them bleed." Rachel held her wrists out to show the scabby sores. "Except for that, he took good care of me. I didn't know he was bringing me to the wagon train. He tried to tell me, but I couldn't understand his language."

"We didn't miss you for hours. Why weren't you with the other girls? You knew how important it was for you stay with the train. We thought you were dead. Your mother nearly went crazy. We searched all over for you but came up empty handed." Her father babbled, as he reached over and hugged his wife and Rachel in one big bear hug.

"I ran after Quincy, but I couldn't find him. That's when the Indian found me. He took me back to the camp, but no one was there. Everyone had gone and left me alone in the wilderness." Rachel wiped away a tear with her grimy finger.

"Somebody get Zeke over here, fast. I want to hear what this Indian has to say," her father called to the crowd.

"Papa, I named my friend, Bearclaw, because of the necklace he wears." Rachel hadn't let loose of his hand while they were talking.

Zeke and Jed made their way through the cluster of friends. Jed gave Rachel a big bear hug and said, "Rachel, honey, its good to have you back from the dead. Me and Zeke here, are going to have a little talk with your friend. You just stand back and listen." The curious crowd circled around Bearclaw, Jed and Zeke, hoping to hear what had happened to Rachel.

"Try to find out what Indian Nation he belongs to, Zeke, then we'll know which language he speaks."

Zeke used his hands in sign language and spoke some guttural sounds. "He belongs to the Ute tribe...traveled from Big Lake...Utah Territory...Mormons...took message to Fort Bridger...treaty...returning to Big Lake...found girl...looked for wagon train...gone...Help me here Jed...Afraid go Fort Hall with child...hang me...ride cross country...find wagons.

"Ask him why he tied her up, Zeke?" Hank asked.

Again Zeke spoke to the Indian. "He was afraid...she'd get lost...forest...hurt or die...wild animals...bad Indians...starve...." The Indian rubbed his stomach as his eyes looked longingly at some biscuits Becky had left on the table after everyone had eaten. "He says he attempted to explain to her that he would try to get her back to her people, and he wouldn't hurt her, but he wasn't able to make her understand." Zeke translated the Indian's dialect.

"Please thank him for me, Zeke, and tell him I named him, Bearclaw." Rachel indicated that Zeke should translate for her.

In sign language and what little Ute he could speak, Zeke related Rachel's message to Bearclaw.

12

"The Brandon family would like to reward you for saving their daughter's life. What would you like?" Zeke added.

Bearclaw looked at Rachel and beamed a broad smile at her, the first one she had seen from the normally gloomy Indian. He looked toward the table with left over biscuits on it, then rubbed his stomach, again. He pointed a bony finger at the biscuits, then pointed to his mouth.

"Better make another batch, Becky. He looks real hungry. I'll find someone to help you," Hank chuckled, as he looked around for a volunteer.

"I'll gladly help," spoke up Lydia Elliott, as she rolled up her sleeves. "The fire's still hot."

Bearclaw squatted on his haunches as he watched the women making biscuits. He greedily stuffed cold biscuits into his mouth. Someone handed him a scalding cup of coffee, then gasped, as he drank it down without flinching. Soon a batch of hot biscuits was ready. As he stuffed one in his mouth, his grimy hand reached for another. He ate until they were nearly gone. Pointing to the fire, then to his stomach, he indicated he wanted more biscuits. Zeke called to Becky, "More biscuits, and hurry, we've got to roll!"

"More biscuits?"

"Yes, more biscuits. Bearclaw asked for more biscuits. It's his reward for saving Rachel. We'll give him all he wants, won't we, Becky?" Zeke patted her on the back, as he unrolled a pack, put a chaw of tobacco in his mouth and began to chew. When things got hectic, Zeke always treated himself to a "chaw" of tobacco. The two ladies baked another batch as fast as they could. As Bearclaw ate this batch his appetite began to slow down. He then stuffed biscuits under his belt and down into the pack on his horse. Seeing that he meant to leave no biscuits behind, Becky wrapped the rest in a dishtowel, tied a string around the bundle, and handed it to the scrawny Indian who must have been nearly starved.

With a happy grin, he patted his stomach and made signs that he was leaving. Jed and Zeke placed a pack of supplies and gifts over his shoulder and made the Indian peace sign with their hands. Rachel walked over to her friend, clasped his hand and walked him to his horse. Quincy danced playfully around the horse on his hind legs, keeping his distance from the horse's hooves. Bearclaw grinned at his silly antics, mounted, looked down at Rachel with a solemn expression on his weathered face. He placed his hand over his heart as his eyes looked deeply into hers, then kicked his horse into motion. Rachel wiped a tear from her eyes as she watched him ride away. She understood what he had told her with that gesture and the caring look in his eyes. A friendship had been born and would never die. They would be friends into eternity!

Becky broke the spell, "Come on, Rachel, let's get you cleaned up and into some fresh clothes. After we clean and doctor those scrapes and scratches, you'll feel a lot better. Then you'll look like our little girl again." Becky's friend, Lydia, had already packed the cooking gear back into the Brandon wagon while everyone else scrambled to get ready for the expected call. Soon it echoed down the line of wagons. "Let's roll!"

"Last call for California," Zeke called as he cantered his pinto pony down the line of wagons. "The rest of us will head out toward Oregon, to try to find the trail through the Snake River Canyons."

The Brandons and the Elliotts were continuing on to Oregon. After a noisy argument with Horace who wanted to go to California, Mrs. Kincaid and Samson won, and they stayed with their friends on the Oregon train. Jed said *HE* wanted to check out California, but Darlin' would miss Rachel and Sarah Ann too much. You never could tell when Jed was "stretching" the truth "just a teensy bit."

Now the emigrants had to get down to serious business, and do some fast traveling. The warning they received at Fort Hall proved to be all too accurate. No road existed! Not even a faint trail. The wagons struggled through a barren, rocky wilderness. Warm clothes were needed to keep out the chill. Men donned heavy coats, and the women brought out their warmer clothes and shawls. The countryside was rough and full of ravines and gullies, dangerous in the frequent rains. The thirsty land drank the water as soon as it fell, leaving everything dry again. Wagon wheels cut deeply into a rocky ridge that was mostly a solid slab of rock. The wagon train made its difficult way through steep walls of stone, while the icy mountain wind blew gusts of frigid air down the emigrant's necks. Sand and sagebrush was everywhere. Sometimes the dust clouds were so thick, the emigrants who were walking, tied a string to the wagon to keep from getting lost. As they worked their careful way down the slopes, the heat returned.

Bandannas, dish towels, and rags were tied around faces to keep out the dust. The Snake River Canyon trail, wound around sharp bluffs and rocky cliffs, that were so narrow they often scraped the sides of the wagons. The rocky, narrow-ledged trail, was so high above the river that it was nearly impossible to get water to slake the thirst of the weary travelers, and their livestock.

The sun reflected off the canyon walls making the temperature rise to nearly 100 degrees. Thirsty animals panted in the heat, and became glassy-eyed with thirst. The roar of the water, over 1,000 feet below, caused some livestock to go berserk and dash over the cliffs to their deaths. Lack of water, alkali dust, heat stroke, and little food, caused many to become sick. Accidents on the rigorous trail plagued the weary train. Several wagons went over the edge and crashed down the sharp cliffs. What little water they had on hand was rationed. Most of the food stores were depleted. Those who had food shared with others. Wood or sagebrush for cooking fires, was scarce.

Further on, no grass for the livestock could be found. The weakened oxen could barely pull the wagons. Some abandoned, broken down wagons were seen strewn across the rocky stretch. Someone had written on the side of one, "Oregon or Bust! Busted by Thunder!" Captain Quarles sent word down the line to throw out all the heavier household items they were carrying to Oregon. "Lighten the wagons. Your life may depend on it!"

Women with bleak expressions on their faces obeyed their husband's edict to abandon even more of their family's possessions in this desolate land. Furniture, chairs, barrels, trunks, boxes, china, Dutch Ovens, and even feather beds, were discarded by the reluctant women. Each article thrown out was tied by a hundred strings of memory. Was it worth this much sacrifice?...Would the Willamette Valley be this desolate?...Could it be, they were being punished for daring to brave this uncivilized wilderness?

Saving what shoes they had left, many chose to go barefoot in this rough land that shredded clothes and leather into bits. Barefoot travelers stubbed their toes, stepped on rocks and cactus, and watched very carefully for rattlesnakes.

One careless young lady was bitten and lay in the jolting wagon with a high fever. The doctor said he didn't know if she would live. Days later, he reported that she would live, but would be very weak for a while.

At night the thirsty, hungry, weary emigrants went to their beds and listened to the sound of wolves howling in the distance. Would this dreadful nightmare never end? The perilous journey along the terrible trail lasted nearly 500 miles.

Sarah Ann was riding in Jonathan's wagon because her feet were cut and bleeding from walking over the rough ground. His father's wagon was first in line, so there was little dust to choke them. Suddenly the dogs that usually ranged out in front began a frantic howling.

"Ro..a..r.r.r!" a terrible sound bounced off the rocky walls.

Frightened, Saran Ann asked, "What was that?"

Again, the horrible noise came, "Ro..a..r.r.r!"

Jonathan's view of the trail ahead was concealed by some crumbled rocks and scrub trees. When the wagon came around the corner, he could see a huge animal standing upright in the middle of the trail.

"Jimeny Christmas!" Jonathan exclaimed, as his eyes bulged! He had never seen a sight like that! That critter was *BIG*! His trembling hand reached under the seat and pulled out the old rifle his father kept hidden there. Excited dogs, not understanding what could happen to them, were circling the snarling, maddened animal.

"Sarah, run after Jed and Zeke. Tell them to hurry. If that animal goes after the oxen, we'll all be caught like a rabbit in a trap! Hurry!" Sarah hiked up her skirts, jumped off the wagon seat, and ran like that ferocious animal was chasing her.

She found Jed and Zeke and some other men prying a broken wheel off an axle. Jed saw her running toward the group and called out, "What's the matter, honey?"

"There's a huge animal threatening the dogs. Jonathan says he could attack the oxen. He needs help! Hurry!" Sarah Ann breathlessly choked out.

Zeke dropped the pole and took off like a flash toward the lead wagon. Jed took a detour to Darlin's side and pulled his old shotgun out of the scabbard. "Now you stay put right here Darlin,' and don't do no nosin' around. That there's an order!" Stuffing several shells in his pocket, he ran as fast as his old legs would carry him. As he passed by Cordelia's wagon he called to Horace, "Now's a good time to tether Samson to the wagon seat. We got us a major emergency here."

A crowd had gathered despite warnings to stay back. Zeke was sighting his rifle in on the bear, hoping to get a clear shot. He had to be very careful, he knew what damage a wounded bear could do. Jed pushed his way through the crowd puffing at the exertion. "Crimeny!" he exclaimed. "I used to could run a mile before I'd get this tuckered!" Gazing at the wild creature slashing at the dogs, he exclaimed in awe, "I reckon if a bear like that one got after me, I wouldn't stop until I reached the Big Ocean. No...siree, Bob!" he cackled with glee.

"Ro...r..r..r..rrrrr!" The angry bear slapped one of the barking dogs with his huge paw. His claws slashed the dog's back. The bloody dog picked himself up and slinked away.

"Ursa Horribilis," muttered Jed to no one in particular.

Zeke whispered quietly in Jed's ear, "Did you say what I thought you did?"

"Yep, a dreaded Grizzly. Lewis and Clark named them when they were out in these parts in eighteen aught five. Sighted lots of them, but had the good sense to stay out of their way. Meanest critter this side of the moon. Don't dare take a shot with that rifle, Zeke, if you wound him, he'll turn into a killer." Jed's eyes glittered as he assessed the situation.

"But, he's blocking our road. We have to do something," Zeke complained.

"Next time he roars, I'll see if I can shoot into his mouth with my shotgun. He's a real big fella, but he's got a tiny brain. That's just about the only way you can kill a grizzly. Lessen you grin him to death like ole Davy Crockett, but I ain't never tried that. Too scared, I reckon," Jed confided. "It takes a real marksman with a buffalo gun to bring down a grizzly. Shore wish my ole buddy Nathanial was here. When he lines up on his target, you can be sure he ain't gonna miss. Finest shot I ever did see."

"I didn't know you were acquainted with Nate. He scouted for this train for a while. As a matter of fact, he's working a train just a few miles behind us. But Jed, I think you should try to shoot for his heart."

"We was good buddies out on the frontier. We wintered together one year."

As the frontiersmen debated the best shot to take, a small brown and white blur came from behind the wagons, straight at the grizzly standing on his hind legs, roaring his wrath. Quincy ran up barking in his shrill voice and nipped the bear, then ran to the other side of the bear and nipped and barked, then dashed away. The bear turned this way and that trying to get close enough to swat his adversary with his claws. The tiny dog dashed in and out, nipping at the bear again and again, and barking in his shrill voice.

"That awful bear will kill Quincy, Jed. Can't you *do* something?" Rachel called, while she wrung her hands helplessly.

"Kaint risk a shot now, honey. I might hit Quincy."

The giant grizzly, standing on his hind legs gave another mighty roar, "Ro...r..r..rrrrr! then dropped down on all four legs, turned and began to amble away. Quincy ran after him nipping and barking. The bear would turn around, snarl at Quincy, then

keep walking away, which delighted the onlookers. The women giggled nervously, the men guffawed and slapped each other on the back. Rachel called to her hero, Quincy, to come back.

"I think it was that shrill bark that did it," chuckled Jed.

"Naw, it was those sharp little teeth," argued Zeke.

"Well, he was brave enough to try *SOMETHING*," sniffed Sarah Ann, looking daggers at Jonathan.

"Gosh, Sarah, I was too scared to move," explained Jonathan sheepishly.

"Me too," echoed Ben.

"I was fixing to take that bear on with my bare hands," bragged Horace.

"Sure is a good thing you didn't try, cuz if that bear didn't wring your fool neck, I would," declared a grinning Cordelia.

Rachel beamed, patted Quincy, then gave him a big hug, "I'm glad Quincy saved us. I was afraid that Darlin' would gallop out next, and attack the bear."

"She would have, but I ordered her to stay put. Onliest time she ever obeyed me. Reckon she was scared, too," Jed explained, choking with laughter, while he scratched under the neck of his red long johns.

That did it. Everyone broke into hilarious laughter. After the tension eased a little, Captain Quarles called, "Back to your wagons, everyone. We've got to get moving. Let's roll!"

13

Half-starved, thirsty, and ravaged by accidents and disease, the wagon train finally wound its way down into the valley, the crooked Snake River ran through. At least, they had water to drink and to give to the thirst crazed livestock. They longed for the food they had wasted along the trail. Menaced by pesky mosquitoes day and night, they wondered how long this nightmare could continue. Sometimes the trail ran into a dead end, so the river had to be forded. Often the wagon beds were caulked and tarred and used as rafts to cross the treacherous river.

Sometimes wagons were roped together to prevent the wild river current from sweeping them away. A few times, chains were used to secure the wagons against the swift river. Even though they tried to keep the loads dry, they were never quite successful. Loads constantly had to be unloaded, dried, and repacked.

Aspen, fir, spruce, pine, green bushes, and shrubs began to dot the land. Soon it looked like a green robe had been carelessly thrown over the hills. As they began to leave the Snake River Canyons behind, they observed pinon and pine covered ridges, stretching on plateau tops in the distance. Towering cliffs, edged with massive boulders, snuggled among the lush green trees.

Soon they observed fish swimming in the river. Attempts to catch the fish were unsuccessful. One day Salmon Falls came into view. Dozens of friendly Snake Indians were spear fishing for salmon that were swimming upstream to spawn. The river was teeming with fish. The struggling salmon were so far from salt water, and had taken so long to reach their spawning grounds, they were poor and flabby and not very nutritious. A very inferior food supply, but much better than they had eaten lately. Several hungry men ran out into the river and began shooting at the fish with revolvers.

The ingenious scouts used hand signs to indicate the hungry emigrants wanted to trade for food. The Indians would swap salmon for almost anything. Hungry pioneers gorged themselves on fresh salmon. A scruffy lot, the Snake River Indians took to begging from the emigrants. At first they wanted guns and ammunition. Pointing to the guns, they would grunt, then point at the dried salmon, indicating they would trade. But, guns were too precious to the emigrants to make such a trade. The only English the Indians could say was, "Bisk?" "Toback?" Unfortunately, most everyone was out of flour by now, and the men weren't about to trade off their precious horde of tobacco. After buying dried salmon with trinkets, to take with them, the emigrants quickly set out on the trail again.

The Captain was worried about the season changing to winter before they could reach their final destination. The slow traveling pioneers didn't have much time left to reach the Willamette Valley before the winter snows began.

Despite the caution taken by the emigrants, wagons and oxen were lost to the river. Several unwary people were injured, and a few died in the perilous crossings. As the month long nightmare trek along the Snake River Canyon ended, the bedraggled members trailed into Fort Boise, near the end of September. The adobe fort belonged to the English owned, Hudson Bay Company (commonly referred to as HBC). Originally, the fort was built for fur trading, but since the trade declined in the 1840's, most of their trade was with travelers on the Oregon Trail.

HBC employees gave the members a hearty welcome by staging a dance for the travel worn emigrants. Scottish men, wearing kilts, danced their native dances to the peculiar sounding music of bag pipes. The busy fort had two acres of land under cultivation and raised sheep, pigs, horses, and cattle. After a brief stopover at Fort Boise, the wagons crossed the Snake River into Oregon Territory.

Descending into the beautiful Grande Ronde Valley, everyone rejoiced at the fresh air and beautiful view. Still nearly 400 miles from their goal, the Captain warned them that they still must cross the rugged Blue Mountains. Then they would pit their skills against the mighty Columbia River.

After the treeless prairie and the stunted scrub trees in the Snake River Canyon, the members were amazed at the tall timber and tangled underbrush that covered the Blue Mountains. An early autumn had turned the mountain leaves to gold, orange, yellow and red. A blue haze hung low over the mountains. The air was cold, the wind sharp and stinging to the face and hands. As they progressed into the rugged mountains, warm breath had to be blown on numb fingers to bring warmth back to them. Tufts of winter brown grass and scattered stones could still be seen among the patches of snow.

Everyone was warned not to wander away from camp. Animals were tightly secured. The trees and underbrush were so thick, that if anyone should become lost, they probably would never be found. The strongest men were selected to cut a road through the wilderness of trees. Many times the emigrants used the lessons learned at Windlass Hill. The grades were so steep, that in order to hold the wagons back, they must use small trees and brush chained to the rear of the wagon. A second span of oxen needed to be used on the steeper slopes. Gaunt and travel weary oxen worked until they nearly dropped. The air was so chilly that the workers raised their faces to the sun for warmth. No one was allowed to rest because they encountered frost at night and a snow storm was threatened.

After reaching the Umatilla River, they must decide which route to take. One route went north to the Whitman Mission. A second route followed the Umatilla to its mouth. The most popular route followed along the foothills west from the Umatilla to The Dalles.

Horace and Cordelia decided to join some other wagons that were going north to the Whitman Mission to rest the oxen, and wait out the winter. Horace joked that his old bones would never make the rest of the trip through the winter cold. The pair felt they would have a better chance at tackling the dreaded Columbia River the following Spring. Cordelia informed her friends that she and Samson had decided to accept Horace's proposal of marriage. As the wagons began to leave the train and their friends, Horace, Cordelia, and Samson wished everyone good speed, and thanked them for all the wonderful help on the trail.

Samson rubbed up against the children's legs and wailed, "Me..o..ow," saying his thanks and farewell in his own way.

The weary travelers were in a pitiful condition. Their clothes and shoes were worn out from the rugged trail. Some were barefoot, and some had bits of canvas or salvaged cloth wrapped around their raw feet to protect them from the cold. The men's faces were weathered and wrinkled from exposure to the elements. Most of the women and older girls had protected their faces, but their hands were red, wrinkled, and cracked. Now, everyone was hungry all the time.

The trail gradually descended down long plateaus. Excited at the prospect of at last viewing the Columbia River, most of the tired emigrants rode in the wagons for the downward slope was easier on the oxen. Nearly all of the men were out foraging for food and had left Jed in charge of the train. Becky was riding with Lydia in the Elliott wagon. Jonathan and his father had gone out with the hunting party. Ben and Rachel were riding with some friends their own age.

Jed rode Darlin' up to the Brandon wagon, tied the mare to the tailgate, climbed through and up onto the wagon seat to sit with Sarah Ann who was driving. He called back to Darlin', "Please don't eat the wagon, these hyar nice folks still need it!" Chuckling to himself, he settled down on the seat and began to clean his fingernails with his knife.

After they had talked about everything they could think of, Sarah, looking thoughtful said to Jed, "Could I ask you a personal question, Jed?"

"Why, sure you can, sweetheart. Ask away."

"I have...uh...personal feelings... for Jonathan. I'm afraid when we get to the river, we'll each go our separate ways and never see each other again. I have crazy dreams of...uh...running away with him. You see Jed, I'm so far from home and I don't have any girl friends my own age to ask." Jed reached over and wiped a tiny tear from Sarah's eye.

"Uh, Sarah, sweetheart, you haven't asked a question, yet?"

"I need to know how I can tell the difference between what's right and what's wrong? I really...uh...really...uh...like Jonathan," Sarah sputtered.

"That there is a question you need to discuss with yore Ma, honey."

"She'll teach me to cook and to sew, but she won't discuss anything personal. She says it's too embarrassing, and I'll find out about all 'that' when I marry."

"I reckon she's got a lot on her mind, right now, Sarah, honey. Here's a little story my Grandma once told me that might help a little. She sat me down after I had gotten into a fight and said, "Jedediah, you must always remember that you have an angel perched on each shoulder. On one shoulder sits an angel from heaven, who whispers good advice into your ear. On the

135

other shoulder sits a fallen angel, who whispers bad advice into your other ear. The good angel's duty is to keep you out of trouble, but the fallen angel's duty is to get you *INTO* trouble. Which one you listen to, is your decision to make. So if you take the wrong advice, you must suffer the consequences."

Sarah Ann was silent for a few seconds, then she whispered, "Good advice, Jed, but how can I tell which is the good angel, and which is the bad angel?"

Jed guffawed, as he reached over and slapped the reins on the oxen to get a little more speed. "That, my dear, you'll have to figure out for yourself. Enough wisdom for today. I've got to go do my duty and check on the other wagons."

Jed climbed back through the wagon and mounted Darlin' who had been waiting patiently. He patted Darlin's neck, then rode around to the front of the wagon, bowed and tipped his hat to Sarah Ann. Smiling, he rode off thinking what a lovely young woman she was. He would have to stop thinking of her as a child. That Jonathan was a lucky rascal, he thought to himself.

That night, they camped in sight of the long awaited Columbia River. Campfires glowed brightly in the darkness of the night. Earlier that day, they had seen a magnificent snow-capped mountain far to the west, before the awesome sunset had brought the darkness. Now, hungry wolves howled in the distance. The foraging hunters had been successful and the emigrants had eaten fragrant venison stew for supper. They headed wearily to their beds, rejoicing at reaching Oregon safely. Feeling sad for all the friends lost along the way, they wondered what tomorrow would bring.

Dawn brought the most glorious sunrise they had ever seen. As the sun began to rise, it glistened off the distant river and cast a luscious pink glow over the pristine snow covered-mountain, far to the west. Men and women emerged from their bedrolls, stretched, and took deep breaths of fresh pine scented air. Captain Quarles called a brief meeting of the men, while the women fixed breakfast from the left-over meat, and the few supplies they had left.

The Captain rode his tall bay stallion up to the waiting men. Some were on horseback and some squatted or sat on dead trees.

"Well, men," The captain exclaimed, as he spat his tobacco juice as far as he could, "we still got a small piece to go. But, this hyar land is part of Oregon. From here we go west to Dalles City, then...."

Jed interrupted, "Uh...Captain...I reckon it's been a spell since you been out this hyar way, but they call the town, 'The Dalles' now."

"You don't say! Anyway, we'll follow down the Columbia River then cross the Shutes River...."

Again Jed interrupted, "Uh...It's a...been renamed ...the... Deschutes River."

With a spiteful look the Captain continued, "Uh..thank you Jed, for that interesting piece of information. Well, that's all I've got to say. This meeting's adjourned!" He abruptly turned his horse and galloped back to the train in a huff.

"Well, I do declare, the cat's got his brisket! He'll be in a 'Blue Funk' the rest of the day. Ain't he a caution?" Jed grinned, as he watched the offended Captain ride away.

Breakfast crumbs had barely been brushed out of beards, or wiped from daintier mouths when a very grouchy call came down the line. "Let's roll!"

Falling into their places in line, the train continued traveling in a westward direction high above the river. Occasional glimpses of the Columbia could be seen. Coming out of the heavy timber at the western edge of the Blue Mountains, they gazed across the upper valley at a glorious Mt. Hood and Mt. Baker with the great Columbia "River of the West" shining in the distance. What a splendid sight! Excited chatter was heard as the train moved slowly along.

Men on horses dashed around frantically, much as they had done when the wagons left Missouri. However, now the picture looked very different. Instead of the horses being fat and glistening with health, their coats were dull and they were thin to the point of being gaunt. The pioneers also portrayed a much different picture. Once plump and glowing with health, wearing nice, clean clothes, they now looked tattered and fatigued. Most wore split and torn clothing, none too clean. Having walked most of the trip on very little food, they had a lean and haggard look about them. Their lagging spirits had been revived after receiving the news they were actually within Oregon Territory boundaries, so they now wore big smiles on their gaunt faces.

A heavy rain the night before left the steep trail slippery and dangerous. The wagons proceeded with caution. Frightening descriptions of the Deschutes River crossing had been passed down through the wagons.

One of the members had been attacked by a mountain lion while traveling single-file through a ravine, and had been severely mauled. Fortunately, a sharpshooter had been riding his horse nearby, and had killed the mountain lion with a quick shot. It was rumored that the luckless emigrant might die. The doctor had explained that because the lion's claws were so filthy, deadly infection would set in most of the time. Unfortunately, the doctor had no medicine to fight infection. Because of the attack, the cheerful feelings the emigrants had felt briefly, were dashed back into despair.

Soon they would discover for themselves the disastrous Deschutes River. Captain Quarles sent word they should reach the river about midday. After their "Nooner," they would begin sending the first wagons across the river. Since each wagon would have to be unloaded and rafted across, it would take considerable time to ford this rampaging river.

The sight of the turbulent river disturbed the weary women and children. Dingy looking Indians stood by, anxious to bargain on a price to raft the wagons across. They began to make camp as they pulled their wagons up near the river. Children scoured the bank for wood. Women built campfires and began to cook their meal with what little provisions they had left. Soon smoke was lifting to the sky and the women began to call encouragement to each other. Visiting together, and the delicious smell of cooking, gave comfort, and the women were soon restored to their former cheerful feelings. Husbands and sons, with the assistance of the scouts, unpacked the wagons and removed the wheels.

The Indians demanded shirts as the price for the crossing. Shirts of any color, fabric or size. Of course the Indians also expected tobacco and trinkets. Money was exchanged for some potatoes the Indians offered. As each man could find a few free minutes, he would grab some food, and eat his meal on the run.

The shrewd Indians had anchored a large raft by a rope on each side of the river. The men placed the four wagon wheels on the raft, then balanced the wagon bed on those wheels. Positioning as much of their supplies as they could around the wagon, they were soon ready to push off. Four Indians stood with long poles, ready to push against the current, as the craft bobbed out into the frenzied river. A shout went up from the emigrants, as they made it to the other side. All afternoon the men kept up the crossings, but not even half of the wagons were across by nightfall. Weary from exertion, the men fell into their bedrolls on both sides of the river. Zeke and Jed had warned them to be vigilant and not let down their guard.

Dawn found the men up, dressed, and waiting for the women to feed them their breakfast, eager to get all the wagons across this morning. Today the weather was overcast, and dark clouds overhead, foretold rain was on its way. There was a chill in the air that had not been there the day before. Some of the men whose horses were skittish wanted to ride them across. The Indians shook their heads and would not allow it.

14

At last it was the Brandon's turn to ride the ferry across. Their wagon and most of their gear was already on the other side. Hank, Rebeccah, and Sarah Ann were waiting on the wet raft for Rachel to board. She looked fearfully at the raft bobbing on the water and shook her head.

"It's alright, honey. Step up onto the raft, you know we have to hurry."

Fearing the dark river and the cold, windy weather, Rachel shook her head again. Terror showed on her face, her eyes looked wild and she clutched her skirt so tightly her hands were white.

"Rachel, come *NOW*!" her father shouted, annoyed at the delay.

Jed approached leading Darlin', and called out to Rachel, "Hey there, honey. Mind if yore old buddy goes across with you? I'm just a mite scared." Reaching out for her hand, he released Darlin's reins, lead Rachel onto the swaying raft, and sat down with his arms wrapped around her. Darlin' looked warily at the swift water twisting around the raft, stepped upon the frail craft gingerly with one hoof, then with a look of reproach at Jed, strode onto the shaky raft.

Jed gave a little secret smile, then winked at Hank and Becky, "I was wondering how I was going to get Darlin' across to the other side. She's so ornery, she only does what she wants to do. I knowed she wasn't about to let little Rachel out of her sight."

As always, accidents happened. It was just too much to ask that the fording could be accomplished without mishaps. An impatient man mounted on his restless horse, refused to wait for his turn on the raft, and was drowned, when the frightened horse panicked. As the horse swam beside the raft, the terrified rider hurriedly tossed his rope to the Indian closest to him on the raft, but the startled Indian was unable to hold on, and the horse and rider disappeared under the swift current. His wife and three small children watched horrified from the bank. A yoke of terrified oxen broke away while they were being unloaded and entangled themselves in the reins, falling back into the river. They could not be rescued. A child's clothing caught fire from one of the campfires. Before anyone could catch the screaming child and smother the fire, her legs were severely burned. An inexperienced boy attempting to ride a skittish horse onto the raft for his father, was thrown from the horse. His head smashed against the corner of the raft. Fortunately, he was alive and the doctor had hopes that he would be alright when he returned to consciousness.

By the time all were across, and the Indians satisfied with their payment, it was too late in the evening to move the wagons. Their stomachs full of thick potato soup, the weary emigrants turned in for the night. Extra quilts and blankets were needed on this very chilly night. Jed looked at the darkened sky and shivered, buttoned the top button on his long johns and thought, "Looks like we're in for some snow!"

Light snow was falling when the wagon train began to move the next morning. Scarves were wrapped around cold heads in an attempt to keep warm. Most everyone was poorly equipped for cold weather. Coat collars were turned up to protect as much bare skin as they could. Bits of cloth were wrapped around worn shoes. By late afternoon the snow stopped falling and a weak sun began to shine. The cold wind continued to blow, making it difficult to keep the fires burning that night. Finally barricades to keep out the wind were erected around the fires.

The next day wasn't much better. The cold wind continued to blow, chilling the emigrants. Several had come down with bad colds. The young lad who had been unconscious, died without awakening. A very brief funeral was held and another rock cairn grave marked the trail from Independence, Missouri.

On the third day of travel the wagons descended the gradual slope to the squalid campground above The Landing, recently renamed The Dalles. The town on the banks of the Columbia River consisted of a squalid camp where a detachment of soldiers bedded down, a blacksmith shop, a general store, two saloons, and a trader's building. Crews of men were cutting trees in the distance. Other crews were hauling trees down to the river. Many men were building rafts, and lashing them together with strips of rawhide or ropes. Smoke from cooking fires fouled the air, causing a haze over the camp. Many people were living out of their wagons while they waited for a raft or a boat to be built. Some lived in tents, and others just slept on a bedroll on the ground. Women were hanging dingy looking wash on improvised lines tied between two wagons.

A lonely looking Indian village stood far away from the camp. Indolent Natives strolled among the pioneers who were tending to their duties. Beggars wandered around asking for "Blue Ruin." Jed had told them to ignore such requests. He said that they were asking for whiskey. Men interested only in making a fast buck, made and sold whiskey to the Indians, destroying their way of life. Children and their dogs romped around playing games, rejoicing to be staying in one place, temporarily, at least. The newly arrived pioneers looked in despair at the sordid camp.

Could this desolate place, be what they had traveled over 2000 miles to reach? This squalid camp at The Dalles, marked the end of the overland trail.

Rafts had to be built to navigate the treacherous Columbia River if they were to reach their destination...the beauti-ful...fertile...Willamette Valley. The camp was already full of hopeful emigrants waiting for rafts to be built. The newcomers had to fit their wagons in wherever there was space. Soon the smoke from their campfires joined the haze that rose above the camp. The weather seemed milder now. At least they didn't feel the cold as much.

Working their way through the maze of humans, animals, wagons and tents, a party of men from the wagon train approached a group of Indians building rafts. Zeke addressed them in an Indian dialect and sign language. Smug looks and laughter met his attempt. He tried in a different dialect, receiving the same response.

Jed stepped forward and tapped Zeke on the shoulder, saying, "Let me give it a try, Zeke." He placed his old shotgun over his shoulder, while he calmly rolled a smoke. Crafty Indians eyes followed every move.

"Have a smoke, gentlemen?" he offered. Reaching out with greedy hands, the Indians eagerly accepted the makings, and began to roll fat cigarettes. Jed pulled out another pack wrapped in waterproofed paper, and selected a wooden match, as if it were a very important decision. Cautiously, he rolled the precious matches back into the pack and placed it carefully in his pocket. He struck the match on the seat of his buckskin pants, watched it flare into flame, then lit the Indian's cigarettes. After they were puffing and blowing out smoke, he lit his own cigarette.

"Now gentlemen, let's have that talk," Jed announced, as he scratched his hairy chest under the red long johns. He began to gesture and speak in an Indian dialect. Zeke could pick up only a few words. When he finished, the Indians replied in a manner that apparently displeased Jed. He spoke again in an agitated voice, his hands moving rapidly. The reply was clearly negative as the Indians were shaking their heads. Jed turned and walked away as the other men followed.

"Dag-nab-it!" Jed exclaimed. "Those varmint eared, rat tailed, sow bellied, fire eating blockheads told me that they won't raft any livestock down the river. They'll have to be sent down the bank of the Columbia River, but, they can't get lost because they'll run into the Willamette River eventually. Whoever goes will have to blaze their own trail. Drat it, Zeke, there's more bad news. There's a long wait for the rafts, and they cost more than most folks can afford. Let's return to the camp, we got a lot of jawing to do."

"But Jed," Zeke reached out and caught hold of Jed's arm, "how in thunderation did you get them to talk with you when they wouldn't talk with me?"

"My old Pa taught me that little trick, bless his soul. He said that when you want to do business, you got to act real friendly, and grease the wheels! I knowed those fellas were mighty fond of tobacco, so I used that for the grease," Jed chuckled, and with a jaunty walk, headed back toward the camp.

This time the men sat around the campfire to hold their meeting. This was not trail talk, but business that involved families. There wasn't much coffee left, but the women got together what they could spare and made a huge potful. Supper that evening consisted of stewed swan, salt salmon, and boiled potatoes. The men had traded some strips of dried elk for the swan. The change in diet was welcomed by all. After supper, Zeke and Jed related the bad news they had received that day. They knew that some could afford the exorbitant price the Indians asked for building rafts, but many more could not.

"Darlin' won't go with the other horses unless I go with her. She says you can't break up a good team." As Jed continued, everyone was laughing, "So me and Darlin' vote to go overland with the livestock. We'll need about five more young fellas. The grownups need to stay to build rafts and help the womenfolk. How about it, boys? Raise your hand if you'll go." Four young boys raised their hands. They were all between eleven and fifteen. Jonathan looked at his parents, then at Sarah Ann, who was pouring coffee nearby. Hesitantly, he raised his hand. Jed looked at Jonathan, nodded his head in agreement, and announced, "Fine, that settles it. We'll take the livestock overland. Pack as much as you can carry on your horse, boys, and bring along a gun and pray you won't need it! We leave early in the morning."

Jonathan's eyes met Sarah Ann's over the glow of the camp-fire. She was standing very still, staring at him as if she had seen a ghost. She set down the heavy coffeepot, dropped the towels she had used to keep from burning her fingers, grabbed up her skirts and ran out of the camp and up the hillside. Jonathan gaped, then looked at Jed with a question in his eyes.

Jed nudged Jonathan with his elbow, and exclaimed, "What's the matter, boy? You got empty space in your head? Better go after her, she might get herself lost!"

Jonathan ran up the hill away from the camp. He searched everywhere for Sarah, but couldn't find her anywhere. He ran farther up the slippery hill, and found her standing quietly beneath some stunted trees, staring at the river in the distance. It was beginning to mist a little and she was shivering with the cold. He walked up to her, took off his coat and placed it around her shoulders. She looked up at him and tried to smile her thanks.

"You're leaving tomorrow. I'll probably never see you again." Her voice quivered a little, although she tried to control it.

"You won't get rid of me that easily, Sarah. I plan on having my own place in the Willamette Valley as soon as I get a little older. Pa promised he'd help me find it. When they open the Territory, there'll be enough land for everybody, and I'll stake out the best land available."

"But you'll be so far away, we'll never see each other!" A lonely tear slid down Sarah's cold cheek.

Jonathan reached over and caught the tear with his finger. "We'll find each other, Sarah. Don't you worry. The Willamette Valley's not that big. I'll find you, somehow." Clasping her cold hand in his, he rubbed her fingers to restore some warmth.

"I know you're much too young to know your mind now, but I can wait. I promise I'll keep the memory of you in my heart forever. Someday when we come of age, we'll meet again. I've heard that love ties will stretch but never break."

The silky mist had stopped and the smiling moon had come out from behind the clouds, highlighting Sarah's wet hair.

"When I find the land I want, I'll need someone to help me raise a family. I can't do it all by my...."

"Yes," interrupted Sarah.

"It breaks my heart to be parted from you."

"Yes!"

"When we're old enough, will you be my wife?"

"Yes!"

"I couldn't bear it if you say no."

"Yes!"

"What?"

"Yes!"

"You're saying...I mean...Yes? You'll marry me...someday?"

"*YES!*"

Jonathan grabbed her off her feet and swung her around as they laughed together.

"Let this bower be our Church and we'll pledge to love each other forever."

"Yes, forever," she answered.

"Forever," he whispered.

"Could I give you a kiss to seal the bargain?" Jonathan asked hesitantly.

Sarah looked down shyly as she nervously twisted her fingers together. "I've got to get back. Pa will be looking for me soon."

With his knees knocking in fright, Jonathan gently put his finger under her chin, tipped her face up so she had to look directly into his eyes. Leaning down, he tenderly touched her lips in a feather kiss. Sarah Ann grinned, tossed his coat to him, picked up her skirts and with her cheeks rosy with emotion, ran back down the slippery trail to the camp.

For a few moments, Jonathan stood silently watching her run, wondering at how fast his world had shifted. Just a few minutes ago he was a lonely young man, wondering about his future. Now, he was practically engaged to be married. Taking off his wet, dripping hat, he tossed it as high in the air as he could. Bellowing his happiness at the waning moon (which he swore later, was smiling), he ran down the slope to the camp to tell everyone the news.

"YA..A.AA..A..H..O.OO..O!"

THE END

AUTHOR'S NOTE:

Those emigrants who finally reached The Landing, later renamed The Dalles, had become accustomed to traveling overland in wagons and now had to learn to build rafts. After fastening their wagons on those frail vessels and waiting for favorable weather conditions, they had to proceed down the treacherous Columbia River. Hundreds of wagon masters sought transportation from the Indian raft builders. Food was scarce, many people went hungry. In desperation, many built make-shift rafts, loaded their belongings, and pushed off into a nightmare! Often icy water was knee deep over the flimsy raft as the wind buffeted them along. Terrified women and their shivering children watched in horror as the menfolk tried to control rafts now at the mercy of the elements. Often rafts broke apart and the trip ended in disaster. Unfortunately, many lives were lost. For those lucky enough to reach safety, soaked belongings needed to be dried out in the sun. Stragglers coming late in the season suffered the rain, sleet and snow that made passage nearly impossible. Many became stranded and were unable to continue their trip and were forced to make camp at The Dalles until the following spring.

Many emigrants stopped at Fort Vancouver and were welcomed and resupplied by Dr. John McLoughlin, Chief Factor for the British Hudson Bay Company. After resting awhile, the settlers would finish their journey by continuing up the Willamette River to their destination, Oregon City, the hub of the Willamette Valley. Many settlers disliked the valley and continued their journey either north across the Columbia River or south into California. Some even took passage on sailing ships and continued on to the Sandwich Islands (Hawaii). A few were so disgruntled at not finding the "land of milk and honey," they turned around and went back to their former homes back East.

Other books written by Cecile Alyce Nolan

OREGON: A FEAST OF DELIGHTS
  Early Northwest Territory history,
  delightful anecdotes, and old family recipes
  that were brought across the Oregon Trail with
  the author's great-grandmother.
  ISBN 0-9633168-0-X
  Library of Congress Catalog Card #92-60522
  Retails for $19.95

OREGON TRAIL MAP
  Depicts the route, describes the landmarks,
  and relates Indian lore. Also gives you the
  feeling of the trauma they experienced.
  ISBN 0-9633-168-1-8
  Retails for $2.95

JOURNEY WEST ON THE OREGON TRAIL
  Retails for $16.95

Distributers carrying books:
  Ingrams
  Pacific Pipeline
  Baker & Taylor
  Sunbelt Publications
  Pacific Crest
  Far West Books

APPENDICES

The following information is presented as an addition to the story for teachers or children who would like to find out more about the Oregon Trail, history of the Northwest Territory, and the people who helped settle it.

Interesting Facts

Historical Places Along the Oregon Trail

Frontiersmen and Information About the West

Indians

Glossary

Bibliography

INTERESTING FACTS

PRESIDENT THOMAS JEFFERSON sent Jefferson Peace Medals along with Lewis & Clark on their Corps Of Discovery Expedition into the wilderness of the far West. On one side of the medallion was a likeness of Jefferson. Two hands clasped in friendship were on the other side. These shiny medals were given to Indian Chiefs along the way to impress them with the "Great White Chief's" power (President Jefferson). Many of these medallions have popped up over the years.

MERIWETHER LEWIS received his medical training from Dr. Rush before the expedition left to explore the Northwest area. The doctor gave Lewis a generous supply of "Dr. Rush's Pills" for constipation. Lewis dispersed these pills for almost any ailment. The brief exposure to Dr. Rush's training was all the doctoring Lewis knew. President Jefferson felt it was adequate for the trip. Only one man died on the 2 year expedition so either they were very lucky or the training was sufficient.

MOUNT ST. HELENS was described in Lewis and Clark's journals as having the appearance of a sugar loaf. In the 1800's, and earlier, sugar was formed into a loaf to be served at table. A sugar pick was used to scratch enough sugar for a serving, then scooped up with a spoon called a sugar scoop. In their journals, the two famous explorers named the beautiful snow covered mountain that rose above the mists, after Baron St.Helens, from England. They could not have been aware that after the glorious white mountain's disasterous eruption, in May of 1980, it would look even more like a white sugar loaf.

SACAJAWEA'S BABY, Jean (Pompey) Baptiste, was born in February. Her labor was hard and long. A fur trader suggested a dosage of ground rattlesnake rattle to hasten the birth. Two rattles was considered an appropriate dose by the bystanders. They were ground and administered. Witnesses swear that within ten minutes she gave birth to Pompey. Truth or Myth? Lewis and Clark's, Corps of Discovery Expedition to the West, left Fort Mandan in April, 1805, accompanied by mother and baby.

FORT VANCOUVER was the civilized center of the uncivilized West. Dr. John McLoughlin was Chief Factor and kept the fort free from attack for more than twenty years. During this time he kept himself and his helpers busy accumulating all the comforts of home. In his orchards grew, apples, grapes, pears, peaches, plums, and figs. They gratefully harvested strawberries, melons, peas, beans, cucumbers, beets, cabbage, squash, and tomatoes.

The fort was comprised of blacksmith shop, bakery, dispensary, Indian trade shop, wash house, Chief Factor's residence, kitchen, shipping office, warehouse and bastion. A high stockade enclosed all the buildings for protection. Outside the stockade were orchards, farms, vast gardens, dairy and livestock barns, bee hives, and houses for the workers.

Many clerks and officers came from the British Isles and were considered "gentlemen." Only the finest silver, china, linens, and glassware were used. Breakfast usually consisted of coffee or cocoa, salt salmon and roast duck served with potatoes, and bread and butter.

For supper: a soup made from duck, tomatoes, vegetables and rice, followed by a variety of meats: roast duck or pork, tripe, trotters, then fresh salmon or sturgeon. A servant replaced the used plate with a fresh plate after each course. For dessert: apple pie or pudding, then another fresh plate with watermelon or muskmelon. After all this, a plate of cheese, bread, and butter was served. Various wines, accompanied by toasts between each course, was the nightly ritual.

The following toast came from Ireland and was probably one that was used for departing visitors:
> "May the road rise to meet you. May the wind be always at your back. May the sun shine warm upon your face, the rains fall soft upon your fields, and until we meet again, may God hold you in the palm of His hand."

Yes, in the early days, Fort Vancouver was truly the "New York of the Pacific!"

LAPWAI MISSION in 1839, had the distinction of having the first printing press in the Northwest Territory.

PLAINS INDIANS lived off the buffalo. They believed "Mother Earth" provided the buffalo so that their family's would have food to sustain them. Tepees, robes, and clothes were made from the hide...glue from the hooves...thread from the sinews...knives and eating utensils from the ribs...water bags from the paunch.

WHITMAN MASSACRE - The dreaded black measles epidemic struck the settlers and the Indian Tribes who lived around the Whitman Mission. Dr. Whitman successfully treated the settlers with his medicine, but the unfortunate Indians had no immunity to the disease. Many died and it was felt that Dr. Whitman and his medicine, that only cured Whites, was responsible. The tribes rationalized that since the medicine cured the settlers, but not the Indians, then the doctor must be giving them poison to get rid of them. A renegade band of Cayuse Indians stole into the Whitman house on November 29, 1847, killing the Whitmans and twelve others. This event touched off the Cayuse Indian War.

HAWKEN RIFLE was accurate at distances up to 200 yards. Powerful enough to drop a buffalo or grizzly bear. It was made by the Hawken Brothers of St. Louis, Missouri. Often a favorite of the frontiersmen.

APPALOOSA HORSE was a descendant of horses brought from Spain. A popular show and cattle horse, it was developed with Arabian ancestry by Nez Perce Indians in eastern Washington State, near the Palouse River.

OXEN can withstand long trips, and are stronger than mules. Indians are not as likely to steal them, since they are slow moving and can be easily tracked. Oxen move approximately two miles per hour. They will continue until they drop, but when they fall down in exhaustion, they usually are unable to get up again.

SANTE FE TRAIL began in 1827 by trappers, merchants, and missionaries going into the Southwest. Independence, Missouri, became the official "jumping off" place because of its woods and available springs which were needed for emigrant campgrounds. By 1848, other towns along the Missouri River were used as starting places for the westward migration. In those days, the Missouri River was considered the frontier and was thickly settled. To support a huge amount of prospective settlers the area must have a proximity to navigation, fertile land, and good water.

FLATHEAD AND NEZ PERCE INDIANS traveled in a group to St. Louis seeking Christianity in 1831. Many religious groups took up the call to minister to the Indians in the Northwest. Often, they would return to the East regaling anyone who would listen, of the "treasures" out West. These reports helped cause the "Great Westward Migration" which is etched in history as The Oregon Trail.

DANGER from hostile Indians, famine, disease, accidents, unpredictable weather, and devastating floods did not deter the hordes of emigrants who came to settle in the Willamette Valley, by the thousands. Each section of the overland journey presented its own difficulties. Despite overwhelming hardships that claimed many lives, the staunch pioneers marched onward to their destinations.

THE OREGON TRAIL was often called the "Marcus Whitman Road" by the emigrants who followed in his footsteps. The Indians named it the "Big Medicine Road."

OREGON OR BUST was the theme of many wagon trains. An example of the feelings of the day: One day, a broken down wagon nearly covered with dust and sand was discovered as the wagon train progressed slowly westward along the trail. Written plainly on the side was, "Oregon or Bust! Busted by Thunder!" Oregon was allowed to join the Union on February 14 (Valentine's

Day), 1859. Free soil Oregon was allowed to join to offset the admission of Texas which was a slave state. The Union upheld a balance between free soil and slave states, which must be preserved.

BLUE BUCKET MINE was discovered in 1845, somewhere in the John Day area in present day Oregon, by emigrants lost and suffering from hunger, cold and thirst. The ill-fated wagon train was led by Stephen Meek, brother of famous mountainman and Sheriff of the Oregon Territory, Joe Meek. Even though experienced, Stephen became lost and the wagon train wandered around trying to find a route to The Dalles. Fact or fable relates that during their journey, some yellow pebbles were found and tossed carelessly in blue buckets. (Manufacturers of buckets in the East confirm that many wooden buckets were indeed painted blue.) After reaching the end of their journey and discovering the pebbles were really gold, the emigrants were asked to disclose the gold's location. They were unable to do so because each of them had been more concerned with their own survival. Truth or Myth?

BEAVER MONEY was minted at Oregon City in 1849. The coin had a replica of a beaver on its face. Formerly flakes of gold were used to barter, but were difficult to measure and wasteful to weigh, so a coin was in great demand even though by this time the beaver had been nearly decimated in the Oregon Territory.

MILITARY FORTS were being built in 1849 to protect the emigrants from Indian uprisings. Earlier fur trading forts had been converted to military forts. The army sent out troops to safeguard emigrants traveling the Oregon Trail.

OREGON PROVISIONAL GOVERNMENT was established at Champoeg on May 2, 1843. The resolution passed 52-50. Soon Oregon City (formerly Willamette Falls), became the capital. (*OREGON: A Feast of Delights*, by Cecile Alyce Nolan, explains the part Joseph Meek played in the passing of that resolution.)

OREGON became official United States Territory in 1848.

CONESTOGA WAGONS were built in Conestoga, Pennsylvania before the 1860's. Experience taught the emigrants that although roomier, this wagon was too big to be easily maneuvered across mountains, rivers, or lowered by ropes.

CHOLERA EPIDEMIC 1849-1853. Cholera was a dreaded disease that took a massive toll along the Platte River. Hundreds died as wagons rolled along the Oregon Trail. The road from Independence to Fort Laramie was called "The Graveyard" and was littered with graves. Bad water was thought to be the cause. Although many cures were tried, few seemed to work. One of the most popular cures was a concoction of cornmeal and whisky.

WAGON TRAIN CORRAL was used effectively to prevent Indian attacks. The wagon train circled, then each wagon stopped with its wagon tongue angled toward the center. Teams were unyoked, grazed, then brought inside the circle. The wagon tongues were then chained together making a safe area for fires and tents inside the enclosure. The wagons provided protection.

BARLOW TRAIL was used as a cut-off to the Willamette Valley by many emigrants. The trail was cleared by Samuel Barlow and Joel Palmer, who later were aided by Philip Foster. The primitive road looped south around Mt. Hood and lead directly to Oregon City, the hub of the Willamette Valley. Balking at the steep prices being charged to raft down the Columbia River and irritated by the long wait, Barlow forged ahead with his search for an alternate trail. The road through the Cascade Mountains was steep and rough and difficult for oxen or mules to travel but nearly impossible for wagons. Named the Barlow Toll Road, a nominal fee of $5.00 per wagon was charged. Cattle and horses were let through for ten cents a head.

INDIANS fighting to protect their lands caused discord on the plains until the railroads came across the nation and the U.S. government placed the Indians on reservations.

VALENTINE'S DAY, February 14, 1859, is when Oregon officially became a state. Slave states and non slave states were used as a trade-off to enter the newly formed Union. Texas was admitted as a slave state so this enabled Oregon to enter the Union as a non slave state.

WASHINGTON became a state November 11, 1889. It took thirty long years after Oregon was admitted to the Union, for Washington to become a state. President Benjamin Harrison issued a Proclamation Of Statehood.

MONTANA became a state in 1889.

IDAHO became a state in 1890.

SOUTH DAKOTA AND NORTH DAKOTA became a Great Sioux Indian Reservation. At that time it was a vast area northwest of Missouri. In 1875, a gold rush commenced in that area and caused difficulties with the Sioux, who did not like Whites trespassing on their sacred lands. By 1883, the continued influx of gold miners and settlers, and the building of the railroad, continued to exert pressure on Native Americans. Many treaties were broken by both sides. The final blow was given when buffalo hunters decimated the immense herds of buffalo. There was no longer enough food to sustain the Indian Tribes.

OREGON WOMEN won the right to vote through the Equal Suffrage Amendment of 1912. This happened eight years before the 19th amendment gave the rest of America's women the right to vote.

CATTLE were often poisoned by eating or drinking something that was bad for them. The following is an old time remedy for cattle poisoning:

one-half pint lard
one-half pint syrup
one-half pint vinegar

Warm lard and syrup and mix well. Stir in vinegar and mix well. Drench cattle immediately.

LIVING MUSEUMS have been set up in many states. A number of positive steps have been taken to help retain sites of historical significance. Our Federal Government, through the National Parks Service, has had the Oregon Trail designated as a National Historic Trail to preserve it for future generations. One hundred and twenty-five more sites are waiting to be preserved. In 1993, the nation celebrated the Sesquicentennial of the Oregon Trail (1843-1993). One hundred fifty years since the Oregon Trail. Most folks are amazed that wagon wheel ruts can still be seen in many places along the famous Oregon Trail.

HISTORICAL PLACES ALONG THE OREGON TRAIL

ST. LOUIS, MISSOURI - Jefferson National Expansion Memorial - This Gateway Arch commemorates the "Gateway To The West!" The Museum of Westward Expansion is open to the public. The park is located on the Mississippi River, near the junction of I-55 and I-70 in downtown St. Louis, Missouri.

SHAWNEE METHODIST MISSION - During the school year, over 200 Indian boys and girls were enrolled. Boys were taught how to farm. Girls were taught how to cook and sew. Both were taught english, spelling, reading, writing, and the rest of the basics. Three buildings are still standing from the 1839-45 period. These are open to the public. During the Civil War, the buildings were used as a barracks for Union Troops. Passing wagon trains often made their first camp nearby, after leaving Independence or St. Joseph, Missouri, for the Oregon Territory.

ASH HOLLOW, NEBRASKA - is located on U.S. 26. The wagon ruts that mark the trail down Windlass Hill are still visible after 150 years. A fine Visitor's Center is located at the Ash Hollow campgrounds where the famous Oregon Trail emigrants made their camp.

COURTHOUSE ROCK, THE POST OFFICE, AND JAIL ROCK, Nebraska - A gigantic rock resembling a courthouse has thousands of emigrant names cut into its surface. Off the main branch of the trail, youthful enthusiasts took side trips to swarm over its surface, and scratch their names to be preserved in time. Historians record it as, "A curious formation of earth near the Platte River." At the Post Office, emigrants left letters written on bleached buffalo skulls for those who followed. The words "Post Office" were cut into the rock. A smaller rock resembling a jailhouse, known as Jailhouse Rock, stood guard nearby. This famous landmark is located off Highway 92, about five miles south of Bridgeport.

CHIMNEY ROCK, NEBRASKA - A National Historic Site. It can be located south of US 26 and the North Platte River, some 23 miles east of Scott's Bluff. Standing alone on the plains, a finger held up in salute to the long gone emigrants, this impressive landmark looks the same as it did years ago. A near-by spring made it a popular camping site. In the 1860's it sheltered a Pony Express station. Later a telegraph and stage station. Chimney Rock is located near Bayard, Nebraska.

SCOTTS BLUFF, NEBRASKA - A traditional hunting ground for Cheyenne, Arapaho, and Sioux Indians. This valley has been a major migration path for thousands of years. Scott's Bluff stands in mute testimony of the passing of hordes of pioneers who viewed the crumbling cliffs in awe. Now a national monument, Scott's Bluff offers the motorist an impressive view of southwestern Nebraska. Located just, off US Highway 26.

FORT LARAMIE, WYOMING - Many of the fort's twenty-two structures have been restored in Fort Laramie's National Historic Site and are open for visitors. Named after an early trapper, Jacques La Ramee, the site at the junction of the Laramie and North Platte rivers in southeastern Wyoming, was an important part of Old West history. In 1843, Marcus Whitman's famous cow column, the first major Oregon Trail migration with nearly one thousand emigrants, stopped for supplies at Fort Laramie. Important treaties were drawn up at Fort Laramie with the Sioux, Cheyenne, and other tribes. This post served briefly as a station on the Cheyenne-Deadwood stage line.

INDEPENDENCE ROCK - This famous landmark is located fifty five miles southwest of Casper, Wyoming, on State Highway 220. "The Great Registry of the Desert" is one of the most famous landmarks along the Oregon Trail. Many believe the rock was given its name in 1822, from a party of mountainmen who camped there on July 4, Independence day. Jedidiah Smith, William Sublette, Jim Bridger, Tom Fitzpatrick, Etienne Provost, Nathanial J. Wyeth, Benjamin L.E. Bonneville, and John C. Fremont, are just a few of the celebrated men who scratched their names on the famous monument. Two prominent names of pioneer women are remembered on plaques. These two valiant White women, Narcissa Whitman and Eliza Spalding, were the first to cross the vast unknown continent.

DEVIL'S GATE, WYOMING - Is a spectacular granite-walled gorge some 350 feet deep and only 30 feet wide at the bottom. The chasm seems to be an inviting notch in a low range of mountains, but the emigrant trains wisely skirted it to the south. Located six miles up the Sweetwater River from Independence Rock.

SOUTH PASS - Roughly mid-way on the trail between Independence, Missouri, and Fort Vancouver. This National Historic landmark stands ten miles southwest on State 28 in Wyoming. The Continental Divide, 7,550 feet above sea level, had other higher and more rugged passes used by earlier fur traders and explorers. Lewis & Clark (1805) crossed the Divide at Bitter-roots far to the northwest. Eastbound, Astoria Fur Trader Robert Stuart's expedition, discovered the pass in (1812) on their return trip. Jedidiah Smith led a party through the pass in 1824. It became the most popular route across the Rockies.

FORT BRIDGER, WYOMING, on Black's Fork of the Green River in southwestern Wyoming, was one of the best known rest stops on the OREGON, CALIFORNIA and MORMON Trails. The few surviving buildings are all from the later military era after 1858. Bypassed by several

159

cutoffs (Sublette Cutoff) which saved many miles, the fort soon fell into disrepair and was sold to the Mormons in 1853. Sublette Cutoff saved about 70 miles, but most of it was desert with no available water. Now a State Historic Site and Living Museum, the renowned fort has displays from the fur trading era through the military period. Located off I-80 on US 30, in the town of Fort Bridger.

FUR RENDEZVOUS at Green River near Daniel, Wyoming. This historic rendezvous of fur trappers in the 1820's and 1830's is celebrated every year in Wyoming's Green River Country. Other historic rendezvous were held at the Popo Agie River, Pierre's Hole, Cache Valley, Bear Lake, and Henry's Ford. Appointed by the American Fur Company for the purpose of trading with trappers and Indians, the event allowed trappers to swap the year's catch of furs for traps, ammunition, tobacco, whisky, and other supplies. The Indians bartered for beads, mirrors, and bright cloth, then used them to trade for their needs with other Indian tribes. After the serious business of trading was finished, the trappers celebrated. They worked out the year's tensions and loneliness by racing their horses, target shooting, wrestling, singing, brawling, gambling, and courting. In 1835, Dr. Marcus Whitman operated on famous mountainman Jim Bridger at a fur rendezvous. Bridger had suffered the pain of an Indian arrowhead imbedded in his back for three years. This heralded operation was one of the major reasons mountainmen agreed to take White women across the mountains and into the Oregon Territory. They held Dr. Whitman in the greatest esteem, but these experienced frontiersmen felt that women in the group surely meant a bad omen. Out of this high regard, Narcissa Whitman and Eliza Spalding accompanied by their husbands, were reluctantly escorted West by grizzled scouts.

FORT HALL, IDAHO - This fort was established in 1834 by Nathanial J Wyeth. With two-thirds of their journey behind them, pioneers could catch their breath, repair their wagons, and decide whether to swing southwest across Nevada to California or northwest along the Snake and Columbia Rivers into Oregon. Today only a marker remains as a reminder of Fort Hall. Long the only inhabited stopping place between Fort Bridger and Fort Boise, the old fort was destroyed by floods. It had been the popular rendezvous of thousands of Indians, French Canadians, Americans, and Spaniards. Fur traders, missionaries, gold miners, homesteaders, and doctors walked or rode past, while others stopped to rest and refresh themselves. Jason Lee preached the first sermon west of the Rockies at Fort Hall, on July 27, 1834. The next day, he officiated at the first funeral, held west of the Rockies, after a man was killed in a horse race.

LAPWAI, IDAHO - On November 29, 1836, Rev. Henry and Eliza Spalding established a mission on (Butterfly Valley) Lapwai Creek. Just 10 miles from present day Lewiston, Idaho. As missionaries to the Nez Perce and Flathead Indians the Spaldings were tolerant and wise in their dealings. Along with religion, they offered reading, writing, agriculture, and home economic instruction. The Spalding Mission Cemetery contains over 100 graves, including those of Rev. Henry Spalding, and his wife, Eliza.

FORT BOISE, IDAHO - A reconstruction of the original fort is located at the eastern edge of Parma a few miles west of US 95. It is filled with displays from the 1834-1855 period. Fort Boise is marked by a monument near the banks of the Snake River, close to the original ford.

THREE ISLAND CROSSING, IDAHO - This major ford on the Snake River, is located just south of Glenns Ferry off I-80. A State Park and campground on the north bank of the Snake River await your visit. A Visitor's Center and swimming beach allow you to camp and play at the same spot the emigrants' enjoyed.

FAREWELL BEND, OREGON - Here the emigrants left the Snake River, often waving farewell to the river that had been so unkind to them, thus giving it the name of Farewell Bend. An Oregon Trail display awaits visitors in a State Park at the bend in the river. It is located four miles south of Huntington on US 30 off I-80.

WAIILATPU, WASHINGTON - More commonly known as the Whitman Mission. A major stopping place for the Oregon Trail emigrants to rest and resupply. In the summer of 1836, accompanied by the Spaldings, Dr. Marcus Whitman and his wife Narcissa, came West over the Oregon Trail arriving at Fort Vancouver. They had been escorted by a reluctant band of mountainmen. On November 3rd, the Whitmans and the Spaldings parted and traveled up the Columbia River to settle on their respective missions. The Whitmans settled at Waiilatpu (place of rye grass) on the Walla Walla River to try to convert the Nez Perce and Cayuse Indians to Christianity. Disease broke out and the Indians felt the Whitmans were causing the deaths. In 1847, some renegade Cayuse attacked the mission and the Whitmans and twelve others were killed. Troops were sent to settle things down and retrieve some captives. Later the tribe handed over the culprits to the law and they were hanged at Oregon City (the seat of the Oregon government). This episode nearly ended the missionary work in the West among the Indians. A National Historic Site is located about seven miles west of Walla Walla, Washington, off US 12.

THE DALLES, OREGON - Named by French Voyageurs (early fur trappers) who thought the great flat rocks in the Columbia River resembled French flagstones, called les dalles. Fur trading forts along the Columbia made The Dalles a rendezvous for Indians and trappers. At The Dalles, travelers were forced to abandon their wagon trains and raft down the Columbia. All

161

livestock was sent to follow the river until they reached the Willamette River, then up river to Oregon City. The trail they followed later became the Columbia Gorge Scenic Highway. The Barlow Toll Road finished in 1846 wended its way around the south side of Mt. Hood and with much difficulty reached Oregon City, the hub of the Willamette Valley, and the end of the Oregon Trail.

FORT VANCOUVER, WASHINGTON - The New York of the Pacific. Site of the British owned Hudson Bay Company's fur trading fort, with kindly Dr. John McLoughlin as Chief Factor. Against British company policy, he rescued and resupplied American emigrants. To the Hudson Bay Company complaints, he replied, "I could not have done more for them if they had been my own brothers and sisters." The fort is located off I-5 in Vancouver, near Mill Plain Blvd exit. The National Park Service has reconstructed some of the buildings and the stockade. It is located just across the Columbia River from Portland, Oregon.

OREGON CITY, OREGON - The official end of the Oregon Trail. The weary emigrants spread throughout the Willamette Valley, establishing farms and setting up businesses. The McLoughlin House, where the good doctor spent his last days, is open to visitors. The "End of the Oregon Trail Interpretive Center" is also open and welcomes visitors. A new Interpretive Center to commemorate the Oregon Trail is now being built, and opens in the spring of 1993.

FRONTIERSMEN AND INFORMATION ABOUT THE WEST

(These entries are listed in approximate date order of the events they represent.)

THOMAS JEFFERSON, America's third president, acquired the Louisiana Purchase from the French Government. Unable to trespass across this huge area while it was French owned, the purchase turned America's eyes westward. The ownership of all the area west of the Continental Divide was challenged by the United States, Britain, Spain, and Russia. To enforce America's presumed ownership, President Jefferson allotted money and formed the Corps of Discovery, headed by Lewis & Clark, to explore and bring back information on the geography, customs of the natives, botany, natural history, and mineralogy. "Manifest Destiny" was the determining factor he used in his decision.

LOUISIANA PURCHASE allowed the exploration of the West. It contained the future states of Louisiana, Arkansas, Missouri, Oklahoma, Kansas, Nebraska, Iowa, South Dakota, and parts of Montana, North Dakota, Colorado, Wyoming, and Minnesota.

MOUNTAINMEN - A mountainman's skin was as dark as a Native American's, due to exposure to sun and wind and winter frost. His hair became long, bushy and dangled to his shoulders. He often tied it back with a rawhide string to keep it out of his eyes. A bristly beard covered his face for warmth in the winter and because he had little time to scrape (shave) his face with a knife. He made his clothes from the hide of a buck deer, or if he was lucky, a doeskin which is much softer. Many were adept at sewing since their lives depended on keeping warm and dry. Often, he could be found using the campfire for light to sew his knee-high moccasins, for he always carried an extra pair. Many of them took an Indian wife to keep them company over the long winters. After he ate his campfire cooked meal, he wiped his greasy fingers on his buckskins to weatherproof them. Around his waist he wore a wide leather belt to hold his knives and pistol. Also, hanging from that belt was a tobacco pouch or a bag holding snuff or chewing tobacco. His bullet pouch was suspended around his neck. Beneath his arm hung a powder horn with all its attachments and cleaning supplies. His rifle was usually carried in his hand or across his pack. Fierce looking beaver traps were carried in his pack. A frontiersman carried no food except coffee, tea, and a little salt. He lived completely off the land. When game was scarce or there was no time to stop and cook, he went hungry. Pemmican was often used as a traveling food. It was a mixture of pounded, dried meat, fat, and berries, carried in a skin bag at his waist. A very high energy food.

BEAVER SKINS were in demand for nearly two centuries. An insatiable demand for beaver gave the fur trapper a booming market. Beaver hats were the height of fashion in Europe and America. Ladies felt their clothes, gloves, hats, and boots absolutely must be trimmed with fur.

ALEXANDER MACKENZIE was the first White man to cross the western wilderness. This daring Scottish fur trader braved the Canadian Rockies overland, to reach the west coast. An employee of the North West Fur Company, he set out to discover the mythical Northwest Passage. He planned to discover the rumored rich fur country and at the same time claim all the promising territory for Britain. Many of his travels took place in 1793, many years before Lewis and Clark's historic expedition across the North American continent. In 1801, Mackenzie left the fur trading business and went back to England to publish a book about his travels, *Voyages from Montreal*. England was unimpressed, but President Jefferson was so fascinated that he sent a copy along with the Corps of Discovery's trek into the vast Pacific wilderness.

MERIWETHER LEWIS was born near Charlottesville, Virginia, in 1774. Appointed to lead the Corps of Discovery, he made a name for himself in history. He was a neighbor, friend, and private secretary to President Jefferson. Lewis possessed the qualities of command that Jefferson was searching for: superb leadership, bodily strength, woodsmanship, an inquiring mind, coolness under stress, and determination. Earlier, he had served in the army on the frontier and understood the Indian Tribes. He was smart and well educated. In 1803, Lewis took many courses so he could learn celestial navigation, geographical and botany information, as well as acquire a medical background. In the spring of 1804, the Corps of Discovery departed on May 17th and reached their winter headquarters, Fort Mandan, near the Knife River in North Dakota. On April 7, 1805, the trip to the northwest wilderness began. The triumphant expedition returned in September 1806, to wild jubilation at their success. They had been gone so long they had nearly been forgotten. It was difficult for the masses to believe that Lewis & Clark could have gone to the far Pacific Ocean, brought back some natives, hundreds of plant and animal specimens, and only lost one man. The party returned to St. Louis, Missouri, after traveling over 7,600 miles of rugged terrain. Jefferson appointed Lewis, Governor of Louisiana in 1806-1809. He died an untimely death in the infamous Natchez Trace in 1809 at the age of 35. While enroute to Washington to edit his journals he stopped for the night at a lonely cabin. Shots rang out and Lewis was found in a dying condition. At first, it was suspected that because he was suffering from depression he had shot himself, but later it was found his money had disappeared. He was thought to be a victim of robbery and murder. The mystery has never been solved.

WILLIAM CLARK was chosen by Lewis, to be his co-captain in their trek through the rugged wilderness. Recruited because he possessed a variety of skills: competent hunter, skilled boatman, and adept at carpentry and blacksmithing. He also possessed a stable character, was self-reliant and was used to harsh discipline. Clark was a Kentucky frontiersman and had been an old Army comrade of Lewis. Clark was a younger brother to the war hero, General George Rogers Clark, who had been a famous frontier fighter in the Revolutionary War. William Clark carved out his own niche in frontier history. Clark wrote most of the famous Lewis and Clark journals, unfortunately, for his spelling was dreadful, often unreadable. Born in Virginia, and just 34 years old, Clark had even more frontier experience than Lewis. The acclaimed Corps of Discovery Expedition took nearly two years to complete. Clark died a peaceful death, unlike Lewis. At his death in 1838, he was honored to be the U.S. Superintendent of Indian Affairs. A true ally to Native Americans.

SACAJAWEA, a Shoshone Indian Princess was companion and guide to Lewis & Clark on their westward expedition in 1805. She was invaluable as an aide to the Pathfinders. Taken captive as a child from (present day Idaho) she had been bought or won as a slave by Toussaint Charbonneau, a French-Indian Interpreter and Canadian fur trapper. Indian tribes along the way accepted the band as peaceful since war parties did not bring women along.

TOUSSAINT CHARBONNEAU was cook and interpreter with the Lewis and Clark expedition. Husband of Sacajawea and father of Jean Baptiste (Pompey) Charbonneau. Later, Pompey and his well known father often were hired as guides.

YORK was Captain William Clark's black servant. Born at the Clark home in Virginia, he had been a life long companion to Clark. Big, strong, and an excellent hunter, he was an asset on the Corps of Discovery Expedition to the Northwest in 1804 to 1806.

CHIEF COMCOMLY (often written as Con-comly) met Lewis and Clark on the lower Columbia river. The one-eyed Chief of the Chinook Tribe was a great help in acquainting the party with the unfamiliar region, and assisting in building a fort to sustain them over the devastating winter. The fort was named Fort Clatsop. The Chief also made friends with John Jacob Astor's fur trading party in 1811.

JOHN JACOB ASTOR had already made a fortune in furs along the Great Lakes. As a German immigrant he was determined to make his mark in this fledgling country. News brought back by Lewis & Clark of enormous quantities of beaver in the Northwest Territory intrigued him. Astor organized the Pacific Fur Company and sent two expeditions to the Pacific. One went by sea and the other traveled overland to the mouth of the Columbia River. In 1811, his agents established a trading post at the site called "Astoria." Later, Astoria became the first town west of the Rocky Mountains.

ROBERT STUART a partner in the Pacific Fur Company, led a small band of men from Astoria back East to report their progress to John Jacob Astor. After a band of hostile Indians stole their horses and supplies, they were stranded and hungry. On October 12, 1812, on foot and searching for an effortless access across the Rockies, they came on a saddle of land with a gentle slope that horses and wagons could manage. This bridge between East and West eventually became known as South Pass, at the southern end of the Wind River Range in Wyoming. Stuart was born at Callendar in Perthshire, Scotland, in 1785, and died in 1848.

JOHN COLTER was a member of the Lewis & Clark expedition. On their return trip, Colter met some men going into the wilderness, who hired him to accompany them on their trip. He asked for a premature departure (discharge) from the expedition. Lewis & Clark could not understand why he would want to return to the wilderness before even finishing the trip he was on, but they agreed and allowed him to go. Lean and sure of himself, this six-foot Virginian, trapped beaver and explored the West for the next four years. His courage was sorely tested in 1808. While trapping with a companion, they were surprised by a large body of Blackfeet Indians. He surrendered, but his fellow trapper resisted and was killed. Bound and stripped of his clothes, he waited while the Indians decided what to do with him. The Chief asked Colter if he was a swift runner. Knowing their ways, he replied he was as slow as a turtle. (In fact, he was well known as being a swift runner.) The Blackfeet cut his bounds and told him to "run for his life" for they would soon follow. Naked and barefoot, Colter sprinted off making for Jefferson Fork, six miles away.

Outrunning all the pursuers except one, he turned, tripped the brave and slew him with his own lance. Exhausted, he reached the Jefferson River and hid under some driftwood until the pursuing, baffled Indians left. After dark he swam five miles downstream, and hit the beach running. One hundred fifty miles and seven days later, he arrived at a fort on the Big Horn River, naked, bloody, starved, dehydrated, blistered, and near death. Miraculously, he survived, and after just a few weeks of rest, he re-outfitted and returned to the wilderness for another two years. Even though he was one of the best frontiersmen, he made little impact because he kept no journals and made no maps to encourage those who followed him into the wilderness.

DR. JOHN McLOUGHLIN was the Hudson Bay Company's Chief Factor for more than two decades. Fort Vancouver, a fur trading fort, was established on the north side of the Columbia River, in 1825. Fort Vancouver was the center of civilization in the Northwest Territory. Many described it as the "New York of the Pacific!" Even though the fort was British owned, only a few residents spoke English for French was the prevailing language. To support its many residents and visitors, extensive gardens and orchards were planted. McLoughlin's kingdom stretched from the Pacific Ocean to the Rocky Mountains, from California to Alaska. He had many names. The Indians called him, "The Great White Eagle," for he had long flowing white hair. In addition he was called, "Lion of the North" or "King of the Columbia." The emigrant's renamed the kindly good samaritan, "Father of Oregon" for the assistance he gave them on their pilgrimage on the rugged Oregon Trail. Fort Vancouver later became a military fort after the beaver was nearly decimated in the northwest. In 1846, McLoughlin resigned and moved to his new home in Oregon City. He was born in the Province of Quebec, Canada, in 1784, and died in the Oregon Territory in 1857.

JEDEDIAH STRONG SMITH was born in 1799, at Jerico, New York. In his early twenties he traveled out West to earn his living as a fur trader, explorer, and adventurer. He was brave, bold, and cool under fire and very outspoken. He considered himself a Christian and his rifle and Bible were his constant companions. Smith explored the uncharted Southwest (Mojave Desert) area twice, and realizing its importance to America, sent reports to William Clark. He left California (Spanish Territory) and explored the West Coast. Devastated after such a long trip and needing supplies, Dr. John McLoughlin supplied what was left of Smith's party, and sent them on their way. While on his travels he encountered a grizzly bear. The menacing grizzly ripped open his scalp above his left eye. The hair never grew back which left him with a receding hair line. In 1830, while in St. Louis, Missouri, Smith made maps of the country he had traveled. In 1832, at the age of 32, he was killed in another foray in the wilderness.

JOSEPH REDDEFORD WALKER was described as having "horse sense" and was a legendary figure in the wild West. He was born in 1798, at Roan County, Tennessee, and emigrated West at a very young age. He believed in Manifest Destiny, and explored and made maps so those who followed into the desolate wilderness, would be well informed. Described as thoughtful, kind, and prudent, he always made sure his men were well prepared. In 1833, Walker was the first man to record seeing the Yosemite Valley. He loved exploring unknown regions. After viewing the Pacific Ocean he found a pass through the Sierra Mountains that later became an entry into California. It was named Walker Pass. The Central Pacific Transcontinental Railroad followed his route through Nevada. Walker felt the acquisition of California from the Spanish was crucial to United States expansion. He gave up the frontier life and went home to Jackson County, Missouri. Elected sheriff, he earned a reputation of being a good lawman and a crack shot. Walker gave up his job to go back into the wilderness as field commander with his friend, Bonneville, on yet another expedition. He was able to look back on a fine career as Army scout, emigrant guide, gold seeker, cattleman, explorer, fur trader, and public servant. Completely blind, he passed away at Martinez, California, at the age of 77. Walker's days of blazing trails were over.

CHRISTOPHER (KIT) CARSON was born in Kentucky, in 1809. A famous western scout, he was an expert rifleman, hunter, and trapper. His deeds were portrayed in dime novels popular in those days. Unfortunately, he could not read about his escapades for he could neither read nor write. Carson accompanied John C. Fremont as a guide over the Rocky Mountains, then later over the Oregon Trail. After he had made a name for himself as a frontier scout, Carson joined the Army, and became a Brigadier-General. Carson died in 1868, honored and famous.

MOSES "BLACK" HARRIS was born in 1800 and became a guide and fur trapper in the early West. He trapped and explored the Rocky Mountains. Harris answered an ad placed in the newspaper asking for young men to go to the Rocky Mountains on an expedition promising riches and adventure. He joined the caravan along with Bridger, Fitzpatrick, and the Sublette brothers. Harris is mostly remembered for serving as a guide to the Whitman-Spalding party in 1836 on their trek to Oregon. In 1844, he helped guide wagon trains on the Oregon Trail. Later, he scouted and lived in the Cascade Mountains. Friendly and well liked, he loved to spin tall tales. Harris died of Cholera, at Independence, Missouri, in 1849.

JOSEPH ROBIDEAUX had the honor of having St. Joseph, Missouri, named after him. As a famous mountainman, he understood the need for trade goods. In 1826, he established a small trading post on what was at that time called the frontier. St. Joseph was a major "jumping off" place for emigrants. In 1849, he established a trading post and blacksmith shop near Scott's Bluff, Nebraska. Robideaux Pass was the major route to the West until 1851 when Mitchell Pass was found to be more accessible.

JOHN BALL was born in New Hampshire, in 1794. He was Oregon Territory's first school teacher. He emigrated to the Oregon Territory with Nathanial J. Wyeth's overland expedition in 1832. Teaching the children at Fort Vancouver was not his favorite pastime. He was also the first farmer to raise a crop for market. Dr. McLoughlin gave him seed to plant when he became dissatisfied with teaching. John caught some wild horses, cut harnesses out of rawhide and taught them to pull a plow. After a long career as a lawyer, he died in 1884, in Michigan.

NATHANIAL JARVIS WYETH was born in Boston, Massachusetts, in 1802. While scouting out West on a geographical trek, he attended the Green River Rendezvous. Unsuccessful at trading supplies with the fur trappers and Indians in 1832, he left the area to travel to the Oregon Territory. Later he built Fort Hall on the Snake River and began trading with the emigrants. In 1834-36, he built a trading post on Sauvies Island called Fort William. Trading with natives, and supervising a fish packing plant kept him busy. Unfortunately, trading competition with the Hudson Bay Company at nearby Fort Vancouver ran him out of business. Prominent in trading, shipping, and exploring, Wyeth died in 1856.

JIM BRIDGER was a mountainman, fur trapper, guide, and far thinking businessman, who helped open the West to the emigrants. By far the boldest of the famous frontiersmen, he claimed to have discovered the Great Salt Lake. At first, he reported that he had found the Pacific Ocean, because the water was salty. Being known as a teller of tall tales, he was disbelieved. Lured into the Rocky Mountains as a hunter in 1823, by an advertisement in the St. Louis newspaper, Bridger left his job as a blacksmith to become one of the ambitious young men to willingly go into the wilderness as a member of the Rocky Mountain Fur company. Later, Bridger showed surveyors the best route for the railroad to take through the mountains to the coast. He was probably one of the most famous mountainmen because of an arrowhead buried in the muscle of his back, that he carried for three years causing him great discomfort. Dr. Marcus Whitman operated and removed it at the Green River Fur Rendezvous. Bridger died on a farm near Independence, Missouri, on July 17, 1881.

CAPTAIN BENJAMIN L.E. BONNEVILLE was an explorer and an army officer. He was born in Tennessee, in 1796. After graduating from West Point Academy in 1815, he made two expeditions to the West in the 1830's while on leave from his Army career. President Andrew Jackson reinstated him and gave him command of a post at Fort Vancouver. By the time he was given the post, Oregon was United States Territory. He was highly honored when Bonneville Dam on the Columbia River was named after him. He died and was buried at Ft. Smith, Arkansas, in 1878.

ZEBULON MONTGOMERY PIKE was a young Army lieutenant in 1806, when he explored the Louisiana Territory. As a guide to Fremont, he took the first wagons over Walker Pass into California. He discovered a high peak and named it Pike's Peak, after himself. Pike was a famous explorer, scout and fur trader.

JIM BECKWOURTH lived among the Indians and won battle honors. He became a Chief. He was born in the South where his mother was a slave. This famous black mountainman, is well remembered for his exploring abilities.

JAMES CLYMAN was a surveyor before becoming a mountainman out West. It was considered an honorable profession and commanded much respect.

After traveling for years, he became a major supporter for the state of California.

HUGH GLASS was a noted frontiersman. A very interesting story is told about his exploits. At one time he was severely mauled by a grizzly bear. He took too long to die, so his companions gave up and left him. The story says he crawled to an Indian village, and lived to tell the story. Truth or myth?

EDWARD ROSE was part black and part Cherokee. It was rumored he had been a bandit and a pirate on the Mississippi River before he became a mountainman. It was reported that he lived in a Crow village and had four wives.

SUBLETTE BROTHERS (BILL & MILTON) Bill had been a constable in St. Charles, Missouri, before he went West to seek his fortune. He beat Wyeth to the Green River Rendezvous in 1833, and sold them supplies, nearly putting Wyeth out of business. Later, he became a partner in the Rocky Mountain Fur Company and ended his life a wealthy man. Milton was little more than a boy when he began his wandering in the far West. A famous cut-off was named after the Sublette brothers. Their many exploits helped settle the wilderness.

BILL WILLIAMS was one of the very first fur trappers, but not as famous as some of the others. He began by exploring the Sante Fe country. At the age of 62, he guided Fremont into the Rocky Mountains. Williams made the wilderness his home for over 40 years.

JAMES (BROKEN HAND) FITZPATRICK was a famous frontiersman. He helped guide Fremont on his second trip West. A partner in the Rocky Mountain Fur Trading Company, his path crossed Walker's, Carson's, Bridger's, and the Sublette Brother's as scout, explorer and tamer of the frontier.

JOSEPH LAFAYETTE MEEK was a mountainman at the age of 18. Born in Virginia, in 1810, he later became a trader and trapper for the American Fur Company. His life became important in Oregon Territory history. He participated in the deciding vote at Champoeg, in 1843. The vote was whether or not Oregon Territory should belong to the United States of America. The "Yays" won. The alternative was to become British Territory. As delegate to Washington, Sheriff, U.S. Marshall, and census taker, Meek lived his full life in support of statehood for Oregon. A very flamboyant character, he loved to dress well, eat well, and enjoy the company of the ladies. Meek loved to tell tall tales. One of his favorites was, when asked how long he had lived in Oregon, he would answer, "Since Mt. Hood was just a hole in the ground." After carving out his niche in history, he passed away in 1875.

DR. MARCUS WHITMAN was a pioneer missionary and physician. He was born in 1802. His vision of the development of the West was a dominant influence in its eventual settlement. He and his wife Narcissa, established Whitman's Mission at Waiilatpu, near Walla Walla, in Washington State. In 1843, the caravans of emigrants brought disease which afflicted the Cayuse Indians. Doctor Whitman's medication failed to make them well. In retribution, in 1847, some renegade Indians rose up and killed the Whitmans and 12 others. Earlier their daughter, Alice Clarissa, the first white child born in the Oregon Territory, drowned at a very young age.

NARCISSA PRENTISS WHITMAN was born in 1808. Missionary, teacher and helpmate for her husband, Dr. Whitman, she was compassionate in her dedication in helping those who were in need. She, with Eliza Hart Spalding, were the first White women to cross the Rockies. Narcissa died at Whitman Mission on that fateful day, in 1847.

REV. HENRY HARMON SPALDING was born in 1803, in New York State. He and his wife, Eliza, journeyed out West with the Whitmans, and settled at Lapwai Mission near the Nez Perce Indians. He and his wife were tolerant in their teachings and instructed the Native Americans in agriculture and home economics as well as religion. Reverend Spalding lived a long and productive life and died in 1874.

ELIZA HART SPALDING was born in 1807. She was a teacher and missionary wife of Rev. Henry Spalding. She crossed the Rocky Mountains with Narcissa Whitman in 1836, on their missionary trip to the Oregon Territory. As the mother of three children she still took time to teach at the Indian School. Eliza died in 1851.

JOHN CHARLES FREMONT was born in 1813, at Savannah, Georgia. He became a military officer, political leader, Western explorer, and map maker. He was fondly called the "Pathfinder." Guided by the famous frontiersman, Kit Carson, he headed West to provide geographic information about the unexplored area. Fremont explored much of the Oregon Trail, sending back detailed reports on the Trail's condition and weather. Assisted by mountainmen Joe Walker and Kit Carson, he charted routes into California and Nevada. Fremont helped California become one of the United States of America. During his distinguished career he was a Senator, a Major General in the Union Army, and Governor of Arizona. Fremont gave his best to his country. He died in 1890, in New York City.

SAMUEL KIMBROUGH BARLOW was born in Kentucky, in 1795. Due to his efforts in 1845, a toll road to Oregon City, that detoured around Mt. Hood, was slashed out of the wilderness. With determination to find a path to take wagons to the Willamette Valley, he explored and made a trail across the

Cascades south of Mt. Hood. Later named The Barlow Road, it saved the emigrants from having to build rafts and brave the perilous Columbia River to arrive at their intended destination. His belief that "God never made a mountain without making a way to get over it" fueled his determination. Barlow died in 1867.

PHILIP FOSTER was born in Maine, in 1805, and became a pioneer, farmer and merchant. He came to Oregon on a sailing ship. Foster established a mercantile store at Oregon City. In 1843, he moved to Eagle Creek and assisted Barlow in his attempt to reach Oregon City with his road building efforts. Portland honored him by naming Foster Road after him. He died in 1884.

GENERAL JOEL PALMER was born in 1810, in Ontario, Canada, the son of an American citizen. As a pioneer leader, he fought in the Cayuse War brought on by the massacre of the Whitmans. With many other gold seekers, he went to seek his fortune at the California Gold Rush. He assisted Barlow in building a new road to Oregon City. Palmer traveled the Oregon Trail twice. After returning to Indiana, he brought his family to settle in Oregon. He make use of the information by writing a guidebook to assist new emigrants on their travels over the Oregon Trail. Later, he became Superintendent of Indian Affairs. Palmer died in 1881.

JESSE APPLEGATE was born in Kentucky, in 1811. Accompanied by his family and over 900 emigrants, he crossed the plains and the terrifying mountains and arrived in Oregon in 1843. He was leader of the famed, "Cow Column." Named so because of the many cows brought along. In 1846, he helped open a new southern route into Oregon named the Applegate Trail. Giving his best efforts to Oregon, he attained considerable prominence in Oregon politics. Jesse died in 1888.

ULYSSES SIMPSON GRANT was born in Ohio, in 1822. He graduated from West Point Academy in 1843. He was stationed at Fort Vancouver, with the U.S. Infantry after it became a military fort in 1852. He was reassigned to California in 1853. Grant became a General in the Civil War and later President of the United States for two terms. After his terms as President, he returned for a brief visit to the Portland area, in 1879. The former president died in 1885.

EZRA MEEKER was born in 1830. He arrived in Portland in 1852, after traveling the Oregon Trail. In 1906, he returned back East over the same route, marking events and monuments along the trail from memory. Credit has been given to Ezra Meeker for the informational signs that newcomers can read along the way. We all enjoy reading Historical Markers. Twenty-first century travelers will still be giving thanks to him in years to come. Meeker died in 1928.

INDIANS

Plains Indian Tribes

The plains culture emerged into full flower with the acquisition of the horse from the South, and the gun from the East. The horse gave the tribes mobility and shaped their quality of life. High social standing was achieved by capturing enemy horses. The gun gave them better access to their main food supply, buffalo meat. As the demand for buffalo hides grew, the flourishing fur trade sounded the death knell for the plains buffalo. The rolling prairie was strewn with decaying carcasses left by professional buffalo skinners.

Free homesteads promised to settlers in the West brought the greedy East-erners across the sacred Indian land. At first, even though the new settlers were crossing land without Indian permission, friendly relationships were usu-ally maintained.

By the mid 1840's, the emigrant movement to Oregon, beginning at Inde-pendence, Missouri, in the early spring of 1843, was a common sight. Distinc-tive white canvas covered wagons traveled the Oregon Trail in long lines. Part of the trail cut across the hunting grounds of the great Sioux Nation, one of the largest and most powerful tribes. The massive influx of emigrants de-stroyed or frightened away game needed to sustain the stable family life of the Native Americans. Professional buffalo skinners killed thousands of buf-faloes for their hides. More alarmingly, the long columns of settlers brought disease to the plains tribes. They had little or no resistance to these diseases and thousands died.

Thus disease, the decimation of their food supply, and the massive emigra-tion of White settlers, were the three major factors bringing a decline of the Indian way of adapting to life on the plains. This new White culture, foreign to them, shifted the balance of power, causing confusion and defiance.

The emigrants used the Platte River as a landmark to the West, and followed it over 300 miles. They crossed out of Nebraska into Wyoming and stopped at Fort Laramie. The indistinct trail cut through the Continental Divide, then followed the Snake River from Idaho into Oregon. The difficult overland trail ended at The Dalles, on the Columbia River. The pioneers determined to reach their destination, the Willamette Valley, learned to build rafts, then braved the treacherous Columbia River in those fragile rafts, hoping to arrive safely. Many did not.

Problems between Indians and the emigrants were increasing rapidly. Pro-tection of both Native Americans and emigrants, became a vital concern of the United States Government, centered in the East. Two major treaties were agreed upon at Fort Laramie in 1851. Another treaty, in July 1853, at Fort Atkinson, attempted to stabilize relations. The Laramie Treaty set up Head

Chiefs more favorable to making peace, and defined boundaries. Unfortunately, these two new treaties caused more discord. Strategic military posts were placed across the plains to keep the peace. Discord ravaged the land.

Eventually the Native Americans were relocated on reservations by the Bureau of Indian Affairs. White Indian Agents were given the responsibility of overseeing the readjustment and care of the Native Americans.

Indian Tribes Closest to the Oregon Trail

APACHES NEX PERCE
ARAPAHOS OMAHAS
BLACKFEET OSAGE
BANNOCKS UTES
CAYUSES PAIUTES
CHEYENNES PAWNEES
CHINOOKS SHAWNEES
COMANCHES SHOSHONES
CROWS SIOUX
KANSAS TETON SIOUX
KIOWA YANKTONAI SIOUX
MANDANS SANTEE SIOUX
FLATHEADS YANTON SIOUX

Northwest Indian Tribes

WALLA WALLAS TENINOS
UMATILLAS MOLALLAS
KLICKITATS KLAMATHS
WISHRAMS MODOCS

Coastal Indian Tribes

KALAPUYANS SWALHIQUA
SILETZ ALSEANS
SIUSLAWANS TILLAMOOKS
 CLATSKANIE
 SALISH

GLOSSARY

- A -

ABANDONMENT - withdrawing, often in the face of danger
ABUZZ - filled with a buzzing sound - busy as a bee
ACCESSIBILITY - capable of being reached
ACCESS - to get at - pass to and fro
ACCOMPANIED - to go with - escort
ACCUMULATION - increase of growth by addition - amassed
ACCUSTOMED - adapted to existing conditions - habit
ACQUAINTED - knew personally
ACQUISITION - something gained
ADEPT - well skilled - expert
ADOBE - bricks made from sun-dried earth and straw
ADORNED - decorating one's person or hat
ADJOURNED - suspended indefinitely or until a later time
ADVANCING - going forward - moving - raising
ADVERSARY - enemy
AFFLICTED - persistent pain - distress
AGENDA - plan of things to be done
AGITATED - to discuss excitedly
AGITATION - to stir up public discussion
ALABASTER - white
ALKALINE - a soluble salty soil detrimental to agriculture
ALTERNATELY - in succeeding turns - every other
AMIABLE - friendly - agreeable - good natured
ANCHORED - secured firmly - fixed
ANGUISH - distress - extreme pain - anxiety
ANTICIPATION - the act of looking forward
ANXIOUSLY - uneasy - brooding - worried - wishing - eager
APPALOOSA - kind of horse with small black patches or blotches on light
  skin
APPENDAGE - something that protrudes from a body, such as a limb
APPLAUSE - clapping of hands - public acclaim
APPRECIATE - to grasp the worth or quality - to value
APPROACHED - accessed - drew close - drew near
APPROPRIATE - suitable - fitting - to take
APPROXIMATELY - close or near - to come close
ARROGANT - thinking one is important - to exaggerate one's worth
ASCEND - to move gradually upward
ASCENT - climb upwards
ASSEMBLED - to meet together

ASSESS - to determine importance, size or value
ATMOSPHERE - the air of a locality - airy
ATTACHMENT - affectionate regard - fidelity
AUGHT - should - zero
AWAYS - slang for close by - not too far

- B -

BABBLED - talking foolishly - prattle - talk excessively
BAFFLED - confused - puzzled
BAG-PIPES - a traditional Scottish wind instrument with reed melody pipes
BALKING - refusing to proceed - contrary
BARTER - something given in trade - carrying on a trade
BASTION - a fortified area or position
BAWLING - bellowing - crying loudly - wailing - lowing loudly
BAY - reddish brown horse with black mane, points, and tail
BEAMED - smiled - grinned
BEDRAGGLED - soiled and stained
BEREAVED - suffering the death of a loved one
BESEECHING - to beg urgently or anxiously
BERSERK - crazed - frenzied - out of control
BIZARRE - out of the ordinary - odd - fantastic
BISK - an Indian word for biscuit
BLEAK - cold - raw - lacking in warmth - not hopeful
BLISTERING - extremely intense or severe - to deal with severely
BONNET - a cloth hat tied under the chin
BRISTLED - standing stiffly erect - to take offense
BROOD - to think gloomily - ponder - meditate
BUCK AND WING - terminology for dance - kick both feet in the air and
  touch them together
BUCKSKIN - a soft pliable cured skin of a buck deer, used to make clothes
BUCKSKIN - a horse of light yellowish dun color with black mane and tail
BUFFETED - battered by the waves or wind
BUXOM - full figured

- C -

CAIRN - a heap of stones piled up as a memorial or a landmark
CALICO - cheap cotton fabric with a floral pattern
CALLUSED - hard thickened skin
CANTANKEROUS - difficult or irritating to deal with
CANTER - three beat stride smoother and slower than a gallop
CANTLE - the upward projecting rear part of a saddle
CARAVAN - a group of vehicles traveling together in a single file

CAUTION - warning - admonishment - precaution
CAULKED - waterproofed the seams - to make tight
CARCASS - a dead body
CHALLENGED - demanded - ordered to halt - disputed - dared
CHASM - a deep cleft in the earth - gorge
CHEMISE - a woman's one-piece undergarment
CHOLERA - a gastrointestinal disease
CHUCK HOLES - holes or ruts in a road
CHURN - a vessel for making butter in which cream is agitated
CHURNED - made butter in a vessel - violent motion
CIPHER - to do arithmetic
CIRCULAR - round - form of a circle - indirect
CLEFT - a hollow between ridges
CLUSTERS - bunched together
COAX - to persuade by means of gentle urging
COLLAPSED - broke down completely - to fall or slide
COMMOTION - an agitated disturbance - noisy confusion
COMPASSIONATE - sympathetic - conscious of others distress
COMPLAINT - an expression of dissatisfaction
COMPLEXION - the appearance of the skin
CONCEALMENT - a place hidden out of sight
CONCLUSION - result - outcome - a reasoned judgement
CONESTOGA WAGON - a large wagon built in Conestoga, Pennsylvania
CONFIDENCE - faith or belief that one will act properly
CONFUSION - the state of being confused - disturbed in mind or purpose
CONSCIOUSNESS - being aware - self-possession - awareness
CONSEQUENCES - effect of own acts - to suffer consequences
CONSIDERABLE - significant amount
CONSOLED - gave comfort
CONSTRUCTED - built
CONTINENT - continuous mass of land
CONTINENTAL DIVIDE - imaginary line dividing the continent from
    Canada to South America - watershed of the North American continent
CONTINGENT - representative group - a delegation
CONTEND - struggle - deal with
CONTRAPTION - device - gadget
CONVENIENT - suitable - proper - handy
CONVERTED - to turn around - changed views - alter - changed
CORRAL - an enclosure made with wagons or vehicles
CORRAL - an enclosure for containing livestock
COVETED - desired - wishing for what belongs to another
CREVICE - a narrow opening resulting from a split or a crack - fissure
CROUCHED - squatted down

CRUMBLING - breaking into small pieces - to fall into ruin

CULTIVATION - tilling the land - loosening the soil to prepare for planting

CURTSY - act of respect consisting of lowering of the body, with a slight bending of the knee

- D -

DAINTIER - choicer - attractive - delicate

DANDER - slang for getting excited

DAUBED - applying a coating in a crude manner

DAWDLERS - spending time idly

DEBRIS - the remains of something broken down

DECIMATED - a large part destroyed

DEPENDABILITY - capable of being depended upon - reliable

DEPLETED - emptied - to lessen in quantity, value or power

DEPRESSION - feeling sadness - dejection - hollow

DESIGNATED - chosen - indicated - specified

DESOLATE - joyless - sorrowful - barren - lifeless

DESCRIPTION - discourse intended to give a mental image

DESPAIRED - lost hope or confidence - despondent

DESPERATION - loss of hope - despairing - extreme measures

DESTINATION - place where one is journeying - where something is sent

DESTITUTE - lacking something needed - suffering extreme want

DETACHMENT - separation - dispatch of a body of troops for a special mission

DETER - to discourage - prevent - inhibit

DETERMINATION - deciding firmly - to carry through an act

DEVASTATED - laying waste - brought to ruin - reduced to helplessness

DIALECT - variety of language - regional - pronunciation

DIGNIFIED - showing self-esteem - reserved in manner

DILAPIDATED - decayed - fallen into ruin by neglect or misuse

DIN - a loud continued noise

DINGY - dirty - shabby - discolored - squalid

DINNER - the principal meal of the day - often mid day

DIRE - dismal - warning of disaster - a forecast - urgent need

DISASTER - sudden calamity - damage or loss - failure

DISCORD - lack of agreement or harmony - strife discord

DISCOURAGED - to deprive of comfort - disheartened - deterred

DISENCHANTED - freed from illusion

DISGRUNTLED - ill-humored or discontented

DISMAL - showing or causing gloom or depression - dreaded

DISMANTLING - taking to pieces - to strip

DISORGANIZED - lacking a system

DISPATCHED - got rid of - set free - disposed of - dismissal
DISPELLED - drove away - scattered - dissipated
DISPENSARY - place where medical or dental aid is dispensed
DISTINCTIVE - serving to distinguish - showing class - worthy
DISTINGUISHED - marked by eminence - excellence
DISTRAUGHT - agitated with doubt or mental conflict - temporarily
   insane
DIVERSIONARY - to draw attention away
DIVISIONAL - being divisive - disagreeable - disunity
DOMINANT - commanding - controlling
DREGS - sediment at bottom - last remaining part
DRENCH - force down the throat of an animal - to wet thoroughly
DROUGHT - a period of dryness - shortage or lack of something
DROVER - one who drives cattle or sheep or horses
DROWSED - to fall into light slumber
DUGOUT CANOE - a boat made by hollowing out a log
DUN - horse with grayish yellow coat and black tail and mane
DUNG - excrement of an animal - manure - repulsive
DURATION - the time during which something exists or lasts
DUST DEVIL - a small whirlwind on land containing sand or dust
DYSENTERY - severe diarrhea with passage of blood and mucus

- E -

EDDY - a small whirlpool running contrary to the main current
EDICT - order - command - public proclamation
ELEMENTS - weather conditions - violent or severe weather
EMBARRASSED - self-conscious - distress
EMIGRANT - a person departing from an area to settle elsewhere
ENCAMPMENT - place where a group is camped
ENCOUNTER - a meeting - sudden often violent clash - combat - chance
   meeting
ENCOURAGEMENT - to give courage, spirit or hope
ENCROACHMENT - to advance beyond proper limits - trespass
ENGROSSED - absorbed - engaging entire attention - occupied
ENTHUSIASM - a strong excitement or feeling
ENTOURAGE - attendants - associates
EQUIPPED - furnished for service or action - dressed - furnished
ESCAPADE - an action that runs counter to conventional conduct
ETCHED - making an impression such as writing in stone
ETERNITY - infinite time - immortality - state after death
EVENTUAL - taking place at a later time - ultimately - resulting
EXHAUSTED - depleted - tired
EXORBITANT - exceeding in intensity, quality, amount or size

EXPERIENCED - made skillful or wise through participation - practiced
EXPECTANTLY - looking forward to something - awaiting
EXPULSION - the art of being expelled - put out

- F -

FASCINATED - bewitched - to command interest - to hold irresistible
  power
FASHIONED - shaped or formed - molded - adapted
FATIGUE - weary - tired
FETCH - to go after and bring back - retrieve killed birds or game
FIDDLE - violin - to play violin - meddle - tamper -to move restlessly
FIDGETY - move with restlessness - nervous movement - uneasy
FISSURE - crack - divide
FLAMBOYANT - strikingly elaborate - ornate - colorful
FLEDGLING - an immature or inexperienced person - one that is new
FLIMSY - lacking in strength - of inferior materials or workmanship
FLINCHING - wincing - recoiling - shrinking from
FLUMMOXED - confused - fooled
FORAGING - hunting for food or equipment - browsing - grazing -
  rummaging
FORBIDDING - prohibiting - inhibiting - command against - to hinder
FORD - to cross - a shallow part of a body of water
FORLORNLY - bereft - forsaken - sad and lonely - desolate - miserable
FOULED - odious - detestable - polluted
FRAIL - easily broken or destroyed - fragile - physically weak - slight
FREAK - to behave irrationally - upset - unusual - abnormal
FRENZIED - temporarily agitated - intense - disorderly
FRESH (cow) - having the milk flow - fill or renewed in vigor and readiness
FRIGHTENED - made afraid - terrified - startled
FRINGED - border of material - strings hanging from a cut edge
FRONTIER - border between two countries - the farthermost limits of
  knowledge
FRONTIERSMAN - one who lives or works on the frontier

- G -

GAUNT - excessively thin - barren - desolate
GAWK - to gape or stare at stupidly
GEOGRAPHIC - belonging to a particular region
GESTURE - motion of the body or hand as a sense of expression
GINGERLY - cautiously or carefully
GLIMPSE - took a brief look - fleeting look
GLISTENED - sparkling - lustrous reflection - glittered

GOSSIPED - person who reveals personal or sensational facts or untruths
GRAZE - to put out to feed
GRIMACE - a facial expression of disgust or disapproval
GRIMY - dirty - soiled
GRISLY - inspiring horror or intense fear - ghastly
GRIT - plucky - persistent - sand - gravel
GRIZZLY - very large powerful bear - found in western North America
GROSS - amount - disgusting - coarse - bulky - 12 dozen - specific amount
GUARANTEE - undertake to answer for the debt - give security to
GUFFAWED - laughed loudly
GULLY - trench worn in the earth by rain or run-off - erosion
GUTTURAL - strange or unpleasant sounds from the throat

- H -

HAGGLING - annoy with bargaining - wrangle - annoy
HALLMARK - an occasion - very important
HARD-TACK - a saltless hard biscuit or bread made of flour and water
HARNESS - gear - equipment - yoke - tie together
HAUGHTILY - proudly - disdainful
HAUNCHES - a squatting position - hindquarters
HAZEL - a light brown to strong yellowish colored eyes
HAGGARD - wild in appearance - worn looking - gaunt
HAZARD - a source of danger - chance - guess as to the outcome
HERALDED - announced - greeted with enthusiasm - publicized
HESITANTLY - pausing in speech - faltering
HILARIOUS - exultation of spirits - merriment - mirth
HITCHED - married - tied the knot
HIT THE HAY - go to bed - retire for the night
HOBBLE - to fasten an animal's legs together - fetter
HOGSHEAD - a large cask or barrel
HOMESPUN - loosely woven - simple - homely - woven at home
HORDES - teeming crowd or throng - swarm
HORIZON - apparent junction of sky and earth
HORRIFIED - feeling horror - filled with distaste - dismay
HOSPITABLE - giving cordial welcome - offering a pleasant area
HOSTAGE - a person held until a promise is fulfilled
HUMANITY - state of being human - mankind
HURLED - pitched - to send or thrust with great force
HURRIEDLY - going speedily - in a hurry - hastily

- I -

IMMEDIATELY - directly - without interval of time - straightway

IMPENDING - near at hand - approaching

IMPROVISED - made - invented - arranged offhand - fabricate out of what is convenient

INCESSANT - unceasing - continuing without interruption

INCIDENT - occurrence - happening likely to lead to grave consequences

INCONVENIENCE - too much trouble or annoyance

INDIGNANT - angered at something unjust

INDOLENT - prone to laziness - sloth

INFAMOUS - having the worst kind of reputation - disgraceful

INFERIOR - lower down - of lower rank or degree

INFLUX - a coming in

INGENIOUS - showing intelligence - clever

IMPASSIBLE - incapable of being passed, traveled, or crossed

INSATIABLE - incapable of being satisfied - quenchless

INSTRUMENTAL - serving as a means - agent or tool

INTRIGUED - interested to a marked degree - tricked - fascinated

INTRUDER - entered without permission

INTERRUPTED - broke - spaced - broke into a conversation

INVALUABLE - value beyond estimation - priceless

- J -

JABBER - talk rapidly - indistinctly chatter - gibberish

JAUNTILY - sprightly in manner or appearance - lively

JAWING - a friendly chat - slang for talking nonsense

JUBILANT - exultant - lively - rejoicing

JUBILATION - an act of rejoicing - an expression of great joy

JUMP THE BROOM - old custom for getting married while waiting for the preacher

- K -

KILTS - a knee length pleated tartan skirt worn by Scottish men

KNOLLS - small round hills

- L -

LAGGARDS - those who lag or linger

LARIAT - a long light rope - lasso

LASSO - rope - to catch or tether

LATHERED - froth from profuse sweating - horse

LECTURED - discourse given before an audience - to reprove formally

LEGEND - a story handed down from the past - popular myth

LEGENDARY - well known - famous - fictitious
LEVER - a bar used for prying - raise or move - bar used to exert pressure
LIQUIDS - to be fluid - flowing freely like water
LOPSIDED - leaning to one side - lacking in balance
LUSCIOUS - having delicious smell or taste - sweet - appealing to the senses
LUXURIANT - fertile - abundant or profuse growth - lush

- M -

MADDENED - crazed - driven mad - enraged
MAGNIFICENT - strikingly beautiful or tasteful - grandiose - sublime
MAGNITUDE - great size or extent - quantity - number
MAJOR - superior in rank - important - greater
MAKE-SHIFT - crude and temporary - substitute
MANEUVERED - moved evasively - shift of tactics
MANGLED - maimed - tearing or crushing wounds
MANIFEST DESTINY - expansion to the Pacific - necessary policy
MANUFACTURE - to make into a product suitable for use
MAULED - beaten - bruised - injured - mangled
MASSACRE - slaughter - to kill a number of beings
MARAUDING - roaming about raiding in search of plunder
MAUVE - a moderate purple, violet, lilac color
McGUFFEY'S READER - popular reading book in the 1800's and early 1900's
MAZE - tangle - network - web - puzzle
MEANDERED - wandering aimlessly - rambled
MENACED - threatened - a showing of intention to inflict harm
MERIT - a praiseworthy quality - virtue - honor - esteem
MILLING - to more around in a circle
MILLRACE - water rushing into a mill with great force
MIMICKED - imitated - simulated - ridiculed
MINTED - making coins - created - produced
MIRED - stuck fast - stuck or sunk in mire
MISERABLE - extreme discomfort or unhappiness
MOCCASIN - a soft leather heelless shoe with a wrap around sole
MOCK - simulated - feigned - imitation
MODESTY - freedom from conceit or vanity - shy - chaste
MONSTROUS - unnatural - gigantic - horrible - abnormal
MOSQUITO - female insect punctures the skin, sucks blood, leaving welts
MURKY - overhanging fog or smoke - vague - obscure - gloomy
MUSCLE - muscular strength - brawn - power
MYSTERIOUS - mystifying - baffling - inexplicable

- N -

NAY - no
NESTLED - to settle or shelter in a house or a nest - to press close
NIGHTMARE - frightening dream - feeling of anxiety or terror
NOMADIC - roaming about from place to place
NONCHALANTLY - an air of easy unconcern or indifference - cool
NOONER - midday meal and rest - term popularized on Oregon Trail
NOVICE - inexperienced - beginner
NUISANCE - one that is annoying - pest - unpleasant
NUTRITIOUS - nourishing - promotes health and growth

- O -

OBSCENE - disgusting to the senses - repulsive - coarse
OBSCURED - indistinct - dimmed - concealed - hidden
OBVIOUS - easily discovered, seen, or overheard
OCCASIONAL - now and then - created for a particular occasion
OCCUPANTS - residing in or on something - residents
OFFENSIVE - attack - nauseous - obnoxious - causing displeasure
OPINIONATED - unduly fond of ones own opinion
OPPORTUNITY - chance for advancement or purpose
OPPONENT - adversary - foe - rival - enemy
OPPOSITION - hostile or contrary action - a body of persons opposing
  something
OPTED - chose - decided in favor of
OMINOUS - foreboding - showing evil - fateful
ORNERY - not acting normally - spoiled behavior - not obeying orders
OREGON TERRITORY - Oregon, Washington, Canada, Idaho, and parts
  of other states
OSNABURG - brand name - a heavy canvas
OUT-RIDERS - mounted attendants - helpers - monitors
OVERWHELMING - extremely upset - overturn - to overpower
OXEN - bovine mammal - an adult castrated male - domestic ox

- P -

PALLET - a small hard temporary bed - tick or mattress
PANDEMONIUM - tumult - a wild uproar
PARCHED - deprived of moisture - thirsty
PASTIME - something that serves to make time pass - diversion
PATIENTLY - slowly and deliberately - willing to bear a problem
PAUNCH - potbelly - the belly and its contents
PECULIAR - strange - odd - curious - different

PEMMICAN - a concentrated food used by the North American Indians - dried lean meat, pounded fine - mixed with melted fat - add to this - dried berries, nuts, or roots and grasses

PERILOUS - hazardous - involving peril

PERISHED - deteriorated - spoiled - died - destroyed

PERPENDICULAR - extremely steep - standing at right angles to the plane of the horizon

PERSPIRING - emitting water through the skin

PERPLEXED - filled with uncertainty - puzzled

PILGRIMAGE - journey

PINTO - spotted horse or pony - marked with splashes of white

PIONEER - first to settle in a region - prepares for others to follow

PITIFUL - compassionate - full of pity - heartless

PLAGUED - calamity - nuisance - hamper - burden

PLATEAU - tableland - level land raised sharply above adjacent land

POSSESSED - to have and hold - own - belong

PRAIRIE - a dry treeless plateau

PRECEDED - previous - foregoing - prior

PRECIPITOUS - very steep - overhanging

PRECIOUS - well thought of - valuable

PREDATOR - one that preys - destroys or devours

PRIMARY - for the most part - chiefly - originally

PRIMITIVE - early stage of development - rudimentary - crude

PRISTINE - uncorrupted by civilization - free from soil or decay - fresh

PROCESSION - moving along in an orderly manner

PROGRESSED - moving forward - advanced

PROMONTORY - a prominent body of land - overlooking lower land or water

PROTRUDING - to jut out from surroundings surface or context

PROVISIONS -a stock of needed provisions or supplies

PROXIMITY - closeness

PRUDENT - discreet - good management of practical affairs

PUNGENT - a sharp biting, stinging taste or smell

PUZZLEMENT - state of being puzzled - questioning - mysterious

- Q -

QUAGMIRE - a soft land that shakes or yields - predicament

QUAVERING - trembling - to speak in trembling sounds

QUEST - to search - pursuit - to make inquiry

QUIVERED - tremor - trembled - shuddered

- R -

RACY - full of zest and vigor
RATIONAL - reasonable - having reason or understanding
RATIONALIZE - to bring to accord with reason - to seem reasonable
RAVAGES - violently destructive effects
RAVINE - a small narrow steep valley - larger than a gully and smaller than a canyon
RAWHIDE - untanned cattle skin
RE-ADJUSTMENT - rearrange - change
REASSIGNED - given another assignment
REBELLIOUS - resisting treatment or management
RECOMMEND - entrust - commit - advise
REGAL - splendid - notable - excellent - magnificent
REINS - straps fastened to a bit by which the driver controls the animal
REINSTATED - placed again - restored to a previous slot
RELUCTANTLY - held back - with great reluctance
RENEGADE - a deserter from a faith, cause, or allegiance - unconventional
REPLICA - close reproduction - duplicate - copy
REPRIEVE - temporary respite - "saved by the bell"
REPUTATION - public esteem - regard - good name
REMUDA - herd of horses from which a choice of mount is made
REPROACH - express disappointment or displeasure
RESERVATION (Indians) - limiting conditions - a tract of public land
RESHOD - to place new horseshoes on an animal
RETRIBUTION - pay back - reward or punishment
RETRIEVED - regained - rescued - salvaged - returned
REVERENCE - honored or respected - adoring
REVITALIZE - to give new life or vigor
REVIVED - becoming active or flourishing
REVOLVER - handgun with cylinders of several chambers
RIGORS - severity of life - austerity - difficult - challenging
RITUAL - ceremony - according to social custom - ceremonial
ROAN - base color - red - black or brown, mixed with white
RUCKUS - row - disturbance
RUMOR - a statement or report without known source

- S -

SACRIFICED - gave up - renounced - sold at a loss - surrendered
SALERATUS - baking substance used instead of yeast
SALVAGED - saved - rescued
SAUCERS - a small shallow dish in which a cup is set at table

SAUNTERED - to walk in an idle or leisurely way - stroll
SCABBARD - a sheathe for a sword, dagger, bayonet, or gun
SCALPED - take a token of victory - remove top part of hair
SCAMPERED - to run nimbly or playfully about
SCATHING - bitterly - severe condemnation - caustic
SCHOONER - a rigged vessel - vessel of the prairie
SCRAWNY - exceptionally thin - slight - lean
SCREECHING - uttering a high piercing scream - outcry of terror or pain
SCRUFFY - unkempt - slovenly
SEE THE ELEPHANT - term meaning explore the unknown - popular on
  the Oregon Trail
SHAGGY - coarse or matted hair - unkempt
SHEATHE - a case or holder for a knife
SHIELDED - hidden by an obstruction - protected
SHREDDED - cut up - torn into small pieces
SHRIEKING - uttering a sharp shrill sound - scream
SIGNIFICANT - having meaning — important - other than mere chance
SINEW - tendon - used as a cord or thread
SKITTISH - easily frightened - frisky - restive
SLICKER - oilskin - raincoat
SLINKED - crept - stole away - moved as in fear or shame
SLOSHING - moving of liquid with a splashing motion
SLUNG - threw - cast - pitched
SMART - mentally alert - bright - (slang) know-how
SMIRK - to smile in a smug manner
SNICKERED - to laugh in a suppressed manner - a horse snorting
SNOOZING - sleeping - napping
SNUGGLED - cuddled - curled up comfortably - to draw close
SOLEMN - gloomy - somber - serious
SORDID - dirty - filthy - wretched - gross
SORREL - light chestnut - brownish, orange, to light brown horse - usually
  with white mane and tail
SPAN - a pair of animals such as mules or oxen hitched together
SPAWN - to deposit or spread out - such as fish eggs
SPECIMEN - an item or part typical of a group or part - piece of a whole
SPECTACULAR - striking - sensational
SPECTATOR - one who looks on or watches
SPIRITED - full of energy - animation - courage
SPRAWLED - to lie or sit with legs spread out
SQUALID - marked by filthiness - neglected - sordid - run down
SQUAW - an American Indian woman - usually used disparagingly
SQUEAKY - a sharp shrill cry or sound - squeal
STALLION - a male horse often used as a stud

STAMPEDED - wild headlong rush or flight of frightened animals
STAUNCH - substantial - steadfast - strongly built
STAVES - narrow strip of wood forming a barrel
STAYS - bone or metal strips used in a ladies girdle
STENCH - stink - foul smell
STRAGGLY - to spread out or scatter
STRATEGIC - necessary to or important to the whole
STRUGGLING - contesting - making violent efforts against
STUNTED - hindering normal growth - development
SUBSTANCE - essence - usefulness - physical material
SUFFOCATING - choking - stifling - impeding - to be deprived of oxygen
SULLEN - gloomy or resentful - silent - pouting
SUPERIOR - higher rank - better - one that surpasses another
SURROUNDED - enveloped - enclosed - encircled
SUSPENDED - ceasing operation - hang - to set aside
SUSTAIN - hold - to give support - keep up - prolong
SWELTERING - overcome by heat - suffering - sweating
SWIVELED - swung or turned swiftly
SYCAMORE TREE - a broad leafed tree native of eastern and central
   North America
SYMPATHIZED - to be in accord, or harmony - commiserate

- T -

TALLIED - reckoned - counted - to list or check off
TARNISHED - to dull or destroy - soil - stain - sully
TATTERED - wearing ragged clothes - torn into shreds - ragged
TAUNTED - sarcastic challenge or insult - tempted - reproached
TEEMING - filled - overflowing - abound - large quantities
TEMPORARILY - during a limited time
TENSION - stress - tautness - pressure
TERRAIN - a geographic area - ground - piece of land
TERRIFIED - scared - filled with terror
TERRITORY - an assigned area - colonial possession
TETHER - a rope or chain to restrict an animal's movement
THREATENING - menacing - uttering threats - warnings
THRONG - a large number of persons - crowd
THUNDERATION - an exclamation showing great feelings
TOBACK - Indian dialect for tobacco
TOLERANT - fortitude - acceptable - indulgent - sympathetic
TORMENTED - distressed in body or mind - distorted - twisted
TORRENTIAL - rushing - tumultuous - outpouring
TORTUOUS - repeated twists, bends, turns - winding, crooked
TRAVERSED - crossing or going across - to pass through

TREACHEROUS - providing insecure footing - marked by hidden danger
TRENCHER - a wooden platter for serving food
TRESPASS - wrongful entry - violate
TRIO - a group or set of three
TRIPE - stomach of a bovine used for food
TRIUMPHANT - victorious - conquering - successful
TROUSERS - pants - slacks - breeches
TROTTERS - slang for pigs' feet used as food
TUCKERED - exhausted - tired

- U -

UNACCUSTOMED - not used to - not usual or common
UNCIVILIZED - barbarous - wild - no proper manners
UNCONSCIOUS - not knowing or perceiving - unaware - no sensations or feelings
UNEVENTFUL - not marked by incidents - placid
UNFORTUNATELY - unsuccessfully - unlikely - regrettable
UNISON - simultaneously - harmonious unison
UNPREDICTABLE - unable to guess - not predictable
UNRULY - not managed or disciplined - willful
UNSCHEDULED - not scheduled - unpredictable
UNSUCCESSFUL - not meeting with success - failed
UNTIMELY - before the due and proper time
UNWARY - easily fooled or surprised - gullible - heedless

- V -

VENISON - edible flesh of wild animal such as deer or elk
VIGILANT - keep watch - stay awake - watchful - alert
VOLUNTEERED - offered oneself for duty or service

- W -

WAGER - gamble - pledge - to lay a gamble - risk
WALLOWED - surge - to roll about
WANED - to decrease in size - dwindle - decline
WARY - aware - attentive - cautious - cunning
WEATHERED - seasoned by exposure to sun and wind
WHINY - a high pitched voice expressing distress or pain - complaining
WHITTLED - to pare or cut of pieces from wood - pare
WIDOW'S WEEDS - black clothing donned after losing a husband to death
WITHERING - a look to cut down or destroy - shriveling
WOBBLY - wavering - staggering - unsteady
WRATH - strong vengeful anger

- Y -

YOKE - to join a pair of oxen together with a wooden frame
YOKE - frame fitted to a person's shoulders to carry a load of two equal portions
YONDER - at an indicated place within sight

- Z -

ZEALOUS - fanatic filled with zeal - fervor

BIBLIOGRAPHY

Parkman, Francis. *The Oregon Trail*. Doubleday & Company, 1964.

Ruth, Kent. *Landmarks of the West*. University of Nebraska Press, 1963.

Havigdhurst, Walter. *The First Book of the Oregon Trail*. Franklin Watts, Incorporated, 1960.

Montgomery, Elizabeth Rider. *When Pioneers Pushed West to Oregon*. Garrard Pub. Company, 1970.

Coons, Federica B. *The Trail to Oregon*. Oregon: Binfords & Mort Publishing, 1954.

Duncan, Dayton. *Out West*. Viking Press, 1987.

Hart, Herbert M. *Old Forts of the Northwest*. Superior Pub. Company, 1963.

Time-Life Books, *The Trailblazers*, New York, 1973.

Lockley, Fred. *History of the Columbia River Valley from The Dalles to the Sea, Vol. I*. S. J. Clarke Pub. Company, 1928.

Snyder, Gerald S. *In the Footsteps of Lewis & Clark*, National Geographic Staff, The National Geographic Society, 1970.

Pioneer Days in Oregon Territory, Compiled from research files of former Oregon writer's projects with much added material, 1956.